No Fire, No Candle

Mary Oldham

PONT BOOKS

First Impression—2001

ISBN 1 85902 945 0

This book is published with the support of the Arts Council of Wales.

Printed in Wales at
Gomer Press, Llandysul, Ceredigion

Stafell Gynddylan ys tywyll heno
Heb dân, heb wely.
Wylaf wers; tawaf wedy.

Stafell Gynddylan ys tywyll heno,
Heb dân, heb gannwyll.
Namyn Duw, pwy a'm dyry bwyll? . . .

Stafell Gynddylan—a'm gwân i'w gweled
Heb döed, heb dân.
Marw fy nglyw; byw mi hunan.

Cynddylan's court is dark tonight,
No fire, no bed;
I will weep awhile—then fall silent.

Cynddylan's court is dark tonight,
No fire, no candle;
Save God, who will keep me sane? . . .

Cynddylan's court—it stabs me to see it:
No roof, no fire.
My lord is dead; myself alive.

Extracts from 'Canu Heledd: The Song of Heledd' from *The Story of Heledd* by Glyn Jones and T. J. Morgan, edited by Jenny Rowland, Gwasg Gregynog, 1994.

I loved you, so I drew these tides of men into my hands
and wrote my will across the sky in stars
To earn you Freedom, the seven-pillared worthy house,
that your eyes might be shining for me
When we came.

T. E. Lawrence, *Seven Pillars of Wisdom*, Jonathan Cape, 1935

All men dream, but not equally. Those who dream in the dusty recesses of their minds wake in the day to find that it was vanity: but the dreamers of the day are dangerous men, for they may act out their dream with open eyes, to make it possible.

T. E. Lawrence, *Seven Pillars of Wisdom*, suppressed introductory chapter, first published 1939

PART I

OXFORD – *RHYDYCHEN*

1

Victoria and Isabel were doing their best to communicate with their new stepsister, but it was hard going.

'What's Welsh for February?' shouted Victoria above the Oxford traffic as the three girls tramped home from school through the stinging sleet, a few weeks before half term.

'*Chwefror*.'

'What?'

She spoke so quietly, and her accent was so weird.

'*Chwefror*.' It came out as not quite a cough, not quite a shiver.

'It sounds just like I feel,' said Isabel valiantly. 'Frozen to death. Ow – watch out!' She pulled her new stepsister away from the kerb as a passing lorry showered them with slush.

'At least you should be feeling more at home, with all this rain and sleet,' said Victoria.

Her new stepsister did not respond. She pulled the hood of her grey duffel coat more deeply over her pale face.

'Joke,' explained Victoria patiently, exchanging looks with Isabel over the duffel coat hood. 'You get fed up with people going on about Welsh rain, I daresay,' she added after a moment.

'It's probably snowing there now anyway,' said Isabel. 'Proper snow, all white and beautiful, not brown and slushy like it always is here.'

'One doesn't come to Oxford for the climate, Isabel,' said Victoria, in an affected accent intended to parody that of their headmistress.

They waited on the edge of the pavement for the pedestrian lights to change. A stronger gust of sleet blew back their new stepsister's hood, momentarily revealing her face before she snatched it forward again. Her mouth was stretched into the polite smile they had come to know. It was a polite, blank, inward smile. It kept them at arm's length.

Victoria and Isabel rolled their eyes at each other. They loitered moodily behind their stepsister as they turned off the Woodstock Road into a tree-lined avenue of semi-detached Edwardian houses.

'Barrel of laughs this is,' muttered Victoria.

'You're telling me, Vix. Weird or *what*? It's been weeks now.'

'You'd think she'd landed from another planet.'

'One with no other people on it. Or at least nobody who spoke English.'

'You'd never believe she was Rhiannon's daughter.'

'*Now* what's she doing?'

Their new stepsister had stopped by the gate of one of the houses and was staring up at a round blue plaque which was mounted on the house wall.

'I mean, why does she always stare at that blue plaque?'

'Pho-one ho-ome,' said Isabel with a snigger.

'I mean, what's so important about Lawrence of Arabia? He wasn't even Welsh, was he?'

'Perhaps she thinks he was a poet like her Dad. Poets have blue plaques put on their houses after they're dead, don't they?'

Their stepsister stopped looking at the plaque. She smiled vaguely in their direction and pulled her hood up again. From inside it she seemed to whisper something.

'What?'

But she was already moving on, heading for the turning into their road, her head turned sideways into the sleet.

'God,' said Victoria. 'I can't stand much more of this.'

'She ought to try harder to get on with us,' said Isabel. 'I mean, who's doing all the work round here, putting ourselves out to be nice and look after her?'

'I wish she'd stop smiling that weird smile,' said Victoria. 'It does my head in.'

'It's the praying I can't stand,' said Isabel. 'On her knees by her bed every night. It's not natural. I mean, I know she's bound to miss her Dad, but praying's not going to bring him back, is it?'

'It's three months now, easily,' said Victoria. 'She ought to get a grip.'

2

'Snow on the Welsh mountains, turning to sleet across the Midlands and the South East,' said the newsreader on the radio as Heledd sat at the kitchen table peeling brussels sprouts for supper while her mother, Rhiannon, grilled sausages and made batter for toad-in-the-hole.

'*Codaf fy lygaid tua'r mynyddoedd*,' quoted Rhiannon, smiling at her daughter. '*I will lift up mine eyes unto the hills.* I always think of that when the weather forecast says snow on the Welsh hills. Your father loved that psalm.' She spoke in Welsh, as she always did to Heledd when there was no one else in the room. When anyone else came in they switched to English.

Heledd smiled and bent over the sprouts. Her face ached with the effort of holding her smile.

'I do wish you'd cry, Heledd,' said her mother, pausing from beating the batter. 'It would do you good to cry, you know.'

Codaf fy lygaid tua'r mynyddoedd, thought Heledd. She made herself translate the psalm into English. *I will lift up mine eyes unto the hills, from whence cometh my help.* The English words are beautiful too, her father had written in his last letter. She thought of the hills, her hills, Yr Arug, Bera Bach and Y Drosgl. Their peaks would be covered with snow tonight, shining white in the darkness. She thought of Craig Wen, the cottage in the hills above the disused slate quarry where she had lived with her father. They had often been cut off when the snow was bad, but it didn't matter. The snow might be up to the window-sills but they were safe and dry inside. The animals too; they would have been brought into the stable which was built on the end of the cottage, right next to the kitchen. She could see them now, the sheep, the goats, the pony, the hens, the cats, all steamy and warm in their beds of straw.

Even in the worst of the snow she could not remember the cottage being cold. She and her father would have built a great stack of dry logs in the chimney recess to feed the fire in the black iron range, and bread would be baking in the old bread oven. Heledd was good at making bread. Her father had taught her. They used to buy flour by the sack and store it in a worn-out chest freezer in the back kitchen, to keep it dry and away from rats. They'd hang the walls with old tapestry blankets and patchwork quilts to absorb the condensation and keep out the draughts. At the other end of the cottage, in the loft, her bed would be pushed up against the chimney breast where the stone was warm from the fire in the little parlour fireplace below.

'Heledd used to have to climb a ladder to go to bed,' her mother had once told her two new stepsisters. They had shrieked with amazed laughter and Heledd had felt humiliated. It was as though her mother was encouraging people to mock at their simple way of life at Craig Wen. Just because *she* didn't like it, Heledd would think. She wants people to think it was primitive and awful so they won't blame her for running away with another man.

Heledd was still angry with her father for not being angry. He had been grief-sticken, but not angry. 'You can't lock a person up in a marriage and throw away the key,' he had said.

'If she loved us, she wouldn't want to go,' Heledd had cried.

'She loves us both,' her father had replied. 'She loves you, and in many ways I believe she still loves me. But I asked too much of her. One day you'll understand, Heledd.'

But before she could understand, he'd died of cancer.

'Sausages!' said Victoria, coming into the kitchen. 'You *know* I don't eat meat.'

'Vegetarian sausages,' replied Rhiannon calmly, pouring the batter over the sausages and onion rings in the roasting tin. 'Open the oven door please, Vix.'

'Why can't we have pasta?'

'You can if you like,' said Rhiannon. 'there's a new packet of spaghetti.'

'It doesn't *matter*,' said Victoria, sitting at the table next to Heledd. 'Ugh, sprouts! I hate sprouts!'

'Well, don't have any, then.'

'Your mother cooks the weirdest food,' Victoria said to Heledd accusingly. 'I mean, toad-in-the-hole! Sprouts!'

'Very nice sprouts,' said Rhiannon cheerfully. 'They came in the organic box this week. I couldn't have grown better myself. Vix, you are looking stressed. Now what is the matter?'

'Nothing,' said Victoria, tilting back her chair and letting it swing to the floor with a bang. 'Nothing at all's the matter. Nothing that a house twice the size couldn't put right.'

'Is she wingeing again?' Victoria's father, David Middleton, came into the kitchen and dropped a stack of cardboard files onto the kitchen unit. He put his arms around Rhiannon, hugging her close to the whole length of his body, and kissing her noisily all over her face.

'Yuk!' said Victoria. 'Must you?'

'Indeed I must,' said David. 'Indeed, I might do it all over again, despite your evident belief that kissing is illegal over the age of thirty.'

'You certainly think it's illegal for the under-twenties,' snarled Victoria. 'You've done it on purpose, don't think I don't realise.'

'Stop it, David,' said Rhiannon, laughing as she

disengaged herself from his arms. 'Why don't you get us a drink?'

'Done what on purpose, baby?' said David to Victoria, stripping the foil cap off a bottle of wine.

'You know!'

'It's been a long day, Vix. Indulge me.'

'Making me share with Iz,' said Victoria, banging her chair legs again. 'It's not fair! I'm the eldest, I should have a room of my own like Virginia Woolf. I'm doing my A levels, aren't I?'

'You do have the use of the study.'

'Yes, when you and Rhiannon aren't using it. Which is all the bl— all the flaming time. The younger ones should share. You should have got bunk beds. I haven't got any private life these days. Justin's getting really fed up, I can tell you.'

'Poor frustrated boy,' said her father, pulling out the cork.

'It's not fair!' Isabel flew into the kitchen, a towel round her shoulders and her newly washed brown hair in rats' tails down her back. 'Just because I'm the youngest, I have to make all the sacrifices. Why should I sleep in a bunk bed? Why did she have to have my room? Why can't she sleep in the loft, if she's so used to climbing up ladders to go to bed?'

'*Isabel!*'

'Well!'

'You know we talked about this, Isabel,' said Rhiannon. 'Victoria.'

'She'd probably like it better,' said Isabel, glaring at Heledd who was looking carefully at the sprout she held in one hand and the kitchen knife she held in the other.

'It's no good, Dad, we'll have to move to a bigger house,' said Victoria.

'We've been through all this before,' said David. 'Find me another fifty thousand quid and I'll be delighted. Do we have to have this conversation every day?'

'You could get a mortgage.'

'We've already got a mortgage, Victoria, quite big enough to be going on with. We had to buy your mother out, remember?'

'We could always move a bit farther out,' suggested Rhiannon, resting her hand on Heledd's head for a moment before carrying the pan of sprouts to the cooker. 'Kidlington, perhaps? Property's a bit cheaper there, I believe.'

'Kidlington!'

Victoria and Isabel watched with fury as their father and stepmother laughed.

'Pass those glasses, Vix,' said David. 'Would you like a drink? Eldest one's privilege?'

'Don't patronise me!' said Victoria, tossing her head.

'Delivered like a pro. But suit yourself.'

'Well, half a glass,' said Victoria sulkily. 'I'm on a diet.'

3

Isabel's bedroom walls were bright pink, with large faded squares where she had taken down her pony and pop star posters. The wardrobe, the chest of drawers and the bookcase were blue, decorated with pasted-on cutouts of flowers and kittens and horses' heads. Isabel had flown into a tantrum when Rhiannon had suggested that Heledd might care to choose some new paint. '*She's* not decorating *my* room!'

Heledd did not mind. It was Isabel's room after all. Heledd's room was the *croglofft* at Craig Wen. If she couldn't be there it made no difference where she slept. If she switched the central light off and the desk lamp on, the room was thrown into shadow. It became less gaudy and strange, so that she felt safer.

Most of Isabel's ornaments and books had been moved except for a copy of *Alice in Wonderland* and a set of the Narnia stories in a slip-case.

'C. S. Lewis lived at Oxford.' She remembered her father telling her that, years ago. 'Before my time, though.'

Her father had been to Oxford University. He had won a special scholarship for Welsh students, so he had gone to Oxford instead of Aberystwyth or Bangor.

'The original Mr Jones of Jesus!' he would say.

He had met Heledd's mother, Rhiannon, at Oxford. She too had been a Welsh student at Jesus College, one of the first women in a college that for centuries had only admitted men.

Heledd could never understand why her father had wanted to go to Oxford rather than a Welsh university. Wales was his country, not England. He had been to prison in defence of the Welsh language. All his poetry was in Welsh.

'Ah, but Shelley went to Oxford,' he would say. 'And Lawrence of Arabia.'

The main thing Heledd knew about Lawrence of Arabia was that he had been born in Tremadog in

Gwynedd, like her father. But he was clearly a famous hero even in England, because the school she was now attending with Victoria and Isabel was called T. E. Lawrence High School.

'Look out for the blue plaque on the house where Lawrence grew up,' her father had written in his last letter. 'Quite near David and Rhiannon's house. I often used to go and look at it.' Her heart had raced, the first time she had seen the plaque. Now it comforted her to pause there every day, knowing that her father must have stood in that same spot, must have walked down that very road along which she now made her way to and from school. It was something to hold on to, a link between her exile and his.

'Some of the best things in my life happened to me in Oxford,' her father had written in his last letter. 'And some of the worst. It will all seem strange and terrible at first, but have faith. Remember what it says in the Bible about needing to lose your life in order to find it. Try to love your new family, for my sake. Trust your mother, and pray for all of us.'

His last letter. His last letter forever.

He asked her to pray, so she prayed. On her knees by her strange bed every night she prayed, and it brought some comfort because it was what she had always done. But as for trusting her mother, how could she? Her mother had betrayed them both. She had left them and run off to England with another man. An Englishman who had been a close friend to both of them at college.

'Well, not entirely English,' she had once heard her mother's new husband protest. 'The Middletons are a Marcher family.'

'Welsh when it suits them,' her father had responded drily.

'Oh, give over, Rheinallt, what the hell does it matter?'

They had laughed, and changed the subject, but Heledd was tormented by memories of such unresolved arguments. She wanted to finish them off, to win the debate on behalf of her father. But her voice had deserted her. For months now it had been slipping away. Nowadays it was an effort to utter the simplest sentence.

'Heledd?'

Her mother came into the room and sat down on the bed. Heledd turned from the window where she had been looking out at the sleet blowing against the street lights. She was getting used to all this bright light at night. The housing estate at Maeshafren, the mid Wales town where she had lived with her aunt during her father's final illness, had been the same. You couldn't see beyond the street lights to the proper night at all. Whereas at Craig Wen the darkness was huge all around you, the endless skies full of stars. They hung so close you could almost pluck them, like cherries from the orchards of night, her father used to say.

'How did things go today?'

Her mother spoke in Welsh. She waited for a moment for Heledd to respond, then continued, 'I've spoken to your form tutor again today. He thinks we can sort out this business of your GCSE syllabus. They can even arrange for you to sit the Welsh medium papers, apparently. He's gone to quite a bit of trouble, Heledd.'

Heledd acknowledged her mother by sitting down next to her on the bed.

'But you'll have to do an awful lot of work on your

own. I'll help you as much as I can, of course, but David's going to see if he can find somebody in college who might like to give you a bit of extra tuition.' She smiled at Heledd's surprised look. 'There are quite a few Welsh-speaking people in Oxford, you know, not just you and me.'

She leaned back on her elbow and regarded her daughter.

'I know it isn't easy, *cariad*,' she said. 'It's a pity this house is so small. And this room is so tiny, there's no room for you to paint.'

A large new box of oil paints, a Christmas present from her new family, sat unopened on top of the chest of drawers.

'At least you've got plenty of work for your portfolio,' resumed her mother steadily. 'Your teacher's very impressed with your work.'

Heledd caught her breath. Her mother had come into the bedroom one day and taken her portfolio of drawings and paintings without asking and shown it to strangers. Her father would never have done that. I should have burned them all before I came, she told herself for the twentieth time. Not just the one.

'They were bad pictures,' she whispered.

'Those lovely landscapes!' said her mother. 'They should be framed. Think how good they'd look hanging on the walls here. They'd remind you of Craig Wen.'

'Isabel would be angry.'

'She'd love them if she saw them. Why don't you show her?'

Heledd shook her head. She stood up, turning her back on her mother, and returned to the window. Outside, a train rumbled cautiously along the railway line that ran along the bottom of the garden. The sleet was turning to snow. Large flakes were blowing against the window, melting on the glass. She felt the warmth of the radiator against her thighs. Perhaps Craig Wen would be quite buried in snow by now. She'd known drifts up to the chimney stacks. But indoors the fire would be lit.

Once again she tried to summon up the picture of the cottage kitchen, warm and cosy in the firelight. Her father would be lighting the lamp and putting jacket potatoes to bake in the oven next to the fire. I'll get the butter, Dad, she called inside her head.

But it was no use. There was no denying the true picture of Craig Wen as she knew it must be at this moment as the snow fell around it. Empty, cold and forlorn. No fire, no candle, like in the old poem. And no Dad, because he lay in the earth in the graveyard of Capel Horeb.

Presently she heard her mother leave the room, closing the door quietly behind her. Heledd waited for a moment, then knelt on the rug and pulled a small, very old, leather suitcase from under the bed. Her art portfolio came sliding out with it and she pushed it back out of sight.

The suitcase belonged to her father, and contained the few treasures she had brought with her from her old home: the six volumes of her father's poetry and essays, an envelope of photographs, her Welsh Bible. And most precious of all, the letters her father had written to her from prison and from hospital during his final illness.

'Why don't you put your things out where you can see them?' her mother had suggested recently. 'We could get some clip frames for the photos.'

'No.' She did not want what was left of her life, her real life, on display for strangers to look at.

She took out the worn brown envelope that contained her father's last letter, and the manuscript of the strange poem he had been working on when he died. Wrapped up in a tissue inside the envelope was a Yale key on a keyring with a minature brass horse shoe hanging from it. The key to Craig Wen. She held it for a moment then put it into the front pocket of her leather satchel, so that she could touch it at any time and be comforted.

She gazed at the remaining contents of the suitcase for a moment, then closed the lid and pushed it back under the bed. She undressed, put on her pyjamas and went to the bathroom to clean her teeth. On her return she knelt once more by the side of her bed, pausing to listen as another train passed in the night, shuttling slowly towards the station. Pressing the palms of her hands together she whispered the Lord's Prayer in Welsh. At the end she added a prayer, as she did every night, a prayer for her father to forgive her.

She had been angry with her father for wanting to send her away to live in a strange city with her mother and her mother's new family. She had been angry and she had done terrible things which she knew had hastened his death. She knew she deserved her exile, and all she could do was to pray for courage to endure it until the time came when she could return home to Craig Wen.

For Craig Wen belonged to her. Her father had left it to her in his will, in the trusteeship of her mother and her aunt Sioned until her eighteenth birthday. After that it would belong to her absolutely, and nothing and nobody would stop her from going back to live there forever.

4

Downstairs, Victoria and Isabel had been joined in front of the living room television by Victoria's boyfriend, Justin, who listened patiently to yet another recital of their feelings about their new stepsister.

'Dad and Rhiannon don't care how we feel,' said Victoria. 'It just amuses them to see how we react to this little cuckoo in our nest. I wish we could go and live with Mum.'

'Ugh, I don't,' said Isabel 'I can't stand Creepy Christopher. Besides, we'd have to share a room there as well, even smaller.'

'They could move to a bigger place, easy,' said Victoria. 'They're earning megabuck money in the City. They could get one of those great big warehouse apartments in Docklands. We'd be near the new Globe Theatre.'

Victoria was doing Theatre Studies as one of her A Levels. Her ambition was to be an actress.

'Oh God,' she said. 'I'd love to live in London. Oxford is so provincial.'

'I hate London,' said Isabel. 'There's nowhere to keep a pony. It's bad enough in Oxford. I wish we lived in the real country.'

'Oh, God,' said Victoria again, jabbing her fingers on the buttons of the remote control so that the television channels jumped wildly. 'Don't you start. Honest to God, Just, you can't get in my room at the moment without falling over model horses. It's driving me bananas.'

'Well, I wasn't going to leave them for *her*,' said Isabel.

'She sounds weird,' said Justin. 'But then, she might think you two are weird as well.'

'Huh!' said Victoria. 'If she's noticed we exist, which I doubt. I don't believe she's spoken to me once. Not once! In fact I haven't heard her speak a single word of English ever since she arrived. Rhiannon should tell her off about it.'

They had got into the habit of referring to their new stepsister as She, and Her. It was her own fault, for having an unpronounceable name.

'She never speaks to me, either,' said Isabel. 'I think she does it on purpose. I don't believe her English is that bad. I mean, this is Britain. Everybody speaks English.'

'Rhiannon should make her talk English,' said Victoria. 'I'm fed up of all this jabbering in Welsh. Every time you open a door, there's Rhiannon talking to her in Welsh. How's she ever going to improve her English if nobody makes her speak it?'

'Perhaps she won't be here very long,' said Justin, taking the remote from Victoria and switching over to *Eastenders*.

'No such flaming luck,' said Victoria. 'She's here for good. She's our stepsister. Where else could she go? She's a member of this so-called family and we're stuck with her.'

'I dunno,' said Justin. 'There's something about her. Those funny eyes she's got. Perhaps she's not a real person at all. I wouldn't be surprised if you wake up one morning and find her bed empty, with only a few white feathers on the carpet to show she's ever been there.'

Victoria and Isabel stared at him.

'Blimey,' said Victoria. 'Have you been reading fairy tales?'

'Just a thought,' said Justin.

'I hope you're right,' said Isabel. 'Then I can have my room back.'

'Besides, didn't she try to burn your uncle's house down, or something?'

'Vix, we weren't supposed to say anything about that,' said Isabel. 'Don't let on to Dad and Rhiannon that you know, for goodness' sake,' she told Justin.

'I don't see why,' said Victoria. 'It's the only interesting thing about her.'

'Come home to a real fire,' said Justin. 'Buy a cottage in Wales.'

'It's not a cottage, it's a castle, practically. One of those fake Victorian jobs with battlements. My uncle was furious.'

'What happened?'

'I think they stopped her before she did any real damage. Pity really, I can't stand him.'

'She can't be all bad, then,' said Justin.

5

'Of course,' wrote Barbara from Maeshafren, '*Wrth gwrs, aeth y bardd Byron i Gaer-grawnt.* The poet Byron went to Cambridge. He kept a bear in his rooms.'

The only person who ever wrote to Heledd from Wales was Barbara Dawes. They had not known each other for very long, but right from the start Barbara had made it clear, in her shy, kind English way, that she was on

Heledd's side. Also, she seemed quite happy to be the one who did all the talking.

'*Ond aeth y bardd Shelley i Rydychen*. The poet Shelley went to Oxford,' wrote Barbara. 'You probably know that. And Lord Peter Wimsey went to Balliol. He played cricket. So my mother's always telling me. Oxford is Mecca as far as she's concerned. Dad says Oxford was all dope and demos when Mum was there in the seventies, but he says nowadays only the rich can afford to go there so it's champagne and heroin instead. But the college buildings look very grand, when you see them on *Inspector Morse*, don't you think? Have you climbed Carfax Tower yet? Or slumbered in the arms of Duke Humfrey?'

Much of this was incomprehensible to Heledd, but she liked the sensation conveyed by the letter of someone jabbering in her ear. Barbara wrote in a mixture of English and Welsh, which she was learning at school. Her Welsh was often clumsy but Heledd was touched that she strove so hard to use it when she could. She knew she ought to write back, but writing was as hard as talking these days.

'How's Barbara?' asked Heledd's mother, watching her from the other side of the breakfast table. She too was reading a letter. Heledd recognised the handwriting on the envelope as that of her Aunt Sioned, her father's elder sister, with whom Heledd had lived during the terrible months of his last illness. Aunt Sioned also lived in Maeshafren. It was where Heledd and Barbara had met.

Heledd passed Barbara's letter to her mother, who began to laugh as she read it. 'She sounds just like your Dad,' she said. 'People in history or characters in books were just as real to him as people in real life. He used to talk about Percy Shelley as though he lived next door.'

She waited for a moment for Heledd to speak, then picked up her own letter again and went on, 'Sioned sends her love. She says she couldn't get up to Craig Wen last weekend because of the snow.'

Heledd did not like her Aunt Sioned. She was always talking about the importance of living in the real world. Heledd sensed that she despised Rheinallt, her younger brother, for not making money, and for going to prison, even for dying of cancer.

Heledd was pleased that the snow had prevented Aunt Sioned from visiting Craig Wen. After every visit she would write complaining about what a nuisance it was, and how typical it was of Rheinallt to put them all to so much trouble over such a dirty, primitive hovel. If she had her way the place would be sold and the money put away for Heledd's education.

'Don't worry,' Rhiannon would tell Heledd. 'I promise that won't happen unless you want it. We're bound to honour your father's will.'

Trust your mother, her father had written. Heledd thought she probably did, in this case. Her mother would not lie to her about Craig Wen. Not intentionally. But in Heledd's worst nightmare a letter from Aunt Sioned would arrive one morning announcing quite cheerfully that she had sold Craig Wen for a good price and they were well rid of it.

She looked at the letter in her mother's hand. It was quite a long letter, but Aunt Sioned's letters always were. Her mother caught her eye and smiled. 'Don't look so anxious, Heledd. I'm sure everything is safe.'

Heledd nodded quickly. 'I must go there at half term,' she said. 'To do the spring-cleaning,'

'Well,' replied her mother, folding up Aunt Sioned's letter and putting it into her jeans pocket. 'We'll see. Perhaps we could all go.'

'No!'

'Come on,' said Rhiannon. 'Why not? Many hands make light work. Besides, the girls would love to see the cottage. Don't you want to show it to them?'

'No!' She glared at her mother, who sighed. 'Heledd, please don't be selfish.'

'They wouldn't like it,' said Heledd. 'There's no bathroom. And they laughed about the ladder.'

She stopped as Isabel came into the kitchen, dressed in a red fleece jacket, tight cream jodhpurs and black jodhpur boots which made her feet look too big for her legs.

'Morning, Iz,' said Rhiannon, switching from Welsh to English. 'Want some toast?'

'No,' said Isabel, sitting down at the table and helping herself to orange juice and cereal. 'No, thanks,' she added as her father came in with the morning paper.

'It's a bit warmer out,' he reported. 'The snow's melting.'

'Iz, if you're going to help with the mucking out you p'raps oughtn't to wear those new jodhpurs,' said Rhiannon. 'It's bound to be terribly muddy today.'

'I'm taking my jeans as well,' said Isabel. 'Miss Wheatley said if I take sandwiches I can stay all day. She could use my help, she said.'

'Now Isabel, you know we're all planning to meet for lunch at the Eagle and Child,' said Rhiannon, moving out of the way as David dropped the paper on the table and poured himself some coffee. 'I said I'd collect you at twelve-thirty, remember?'

'It wouldn't matter if I didn't go,' said Isabel. 'It's boring anyway.' She kept her eyes on her cereal as she spoke, spooning it quickly into her mouth.

'You're coming,' said David. 'No more argument.'

'It's not fair!' said Isabel. 'You won't let me go riding every week, and then when I get the chance to stay all day for free you won't let me do that either! If I don't stay today, Miss Wheatley won't ask me again!'

'Hard cheese,' said David, sorting through the Saturday supplements and opening the Review section.

'Mum would let me,' said Isabel.

'I doubt it. She doesn't want a horsy bore for a daughter any more than I do.'

Isabel's eyes filled with tears. She glared across the table at Heledd. 'This is all your fault,' she said. 'We only have to go to this horrible old pub because you've never been there. Everything we do is organised for you.'

'Oh yes? And Rhiannon's taxi service to and from the stables is for Heledd's benefit too, is it?'

'Just this time, Iz,' said Rhiannon in coaxing tones. 'Vix is coming too. It wouldn't be the same without you.'

'But this is my big chance! I'll never get asked again!'

'I'm sure you will,' said Rhiannon. 'I shall have a word with Miss Wheatley myself. I'm sure she'll understand.'

Heledd said nothing. She did not see why Isabel should not spend all day at the riding stables if that was what she wanted. It was what she would have wanted to do herself, if she had been at school all week with no animals to look after.

At Craig Wen, there had always been animals. If she were there now she would already have fed the hens, collected the eggs, milked Sali the goat and filled a fresh haynet for Shani, the white Welsh mountain pony mare who lived at Craig Wen in retirement. How lovely it would be to be there now, eating her breakfast with her father and planning a morning clearing the snow from the yard, like last year when they had harnessed Shani to a sledge her father had made from an old door.

Heledd thought of Shani, remembering her white whiskers and the thick coat she would grow every winter. In the spring it would rub off on every thistle or fence post. All the birds' nests in the area had soft white linings made from Shani's winter coat.

Like all the other animals, Shani had been given to the Davies family at Tanygraig, the neighbouring farm, when Heledd and her father had had to leave Craig Wen. Since then Heledd had had no animal to care for. She had not even ridden, except for those few times she had borrowed her friend Barbara's pony, another white mare called Bianca. But Heledd had shut away the memory of her last ride on Bianca, because it had ended so unbearably.

'That's no good,' Isabel was saying. 'It was today Miss Wheatley needed the help. I promised.' She looked cautiously at her father, who looked over the top of the paper and said, 'Shut up, Iz, for pity's sake.'

Isabel's bottom lip trembled. Rhiannon said quickly, 'I'm sure if I have a word with Miss Wheatley she'll understand. You shouldn't really make promises of that sort without checking with us, you know.' Isabel drew breath to reply but Rhiannon continued, 'Heledd might like to go riding with you one day. She's used to horses.'

A look of horror came over Isabel's face.

Heledd shook her head vehemently. If she never rode a pony again, she wouldn't care.

'She doesn't want to,' said Isabel. 'Anyway there wouldn't be anybody for her to talk Welsh to. So can we go? I need to be at the stables by nine-thirty, especially if I'm not going to be allowed to stay all day.'

'Your taxi will be waiting,' replied Rhiannon with a dry smile.

'Isabel,' said David from behind the paper. 'Mind your tone.' He looked up at Rhiannon, and she moved round the table to stand behind him with her hands on his shoulders. Heledd scraped back her chair. As she stood up Victoria swung into the room through the open door.

'Oh, God,' she said, 'I'm late.' She poured herself a glass of orange juice and drank it. 'I'm off. See you later.'

Victoria had a Saturday morning job as a waitress at the Road to Damascus Cafè in Jericho, a favourite haunt of her friends in the sixth form. Rhiannon had helped her to persuade her father that having a Saturday job would not cause her to neglect her A Level work.

'Don't work too hard,' said her father now. 'We'll see you at one.'

'They might want me to stay on for an hour if they're busy,' said Victoria.

'One o'clock,' repeated her father.

'All *right*. Ye gods, perhaps one day I'll be old enough to be allowed to spend *all day* with my own friends.'

'Bring them along, if you like,' said Rhiannon.

'Not likely,' said Victoria. 'They're all in love with you. The guys anyway. I don't get a look in. Ta-ra for now.'

The front door slammed. David winced.

'What a face, you old fogey,' Rhiannon told him, kissing the top of his head. 'Heledd, leave the dishes. I'll stack the dishwasher later. Iz, you nip and clean your teeth while I start the car. Have you got your crash cap?'

'Safety helmet,' corrected Isabel, sounding much more cheerful.

'Sorry,' said Rhiannon. 'It was always crash caps in the pony books I used to read. Now then, what about your gloves and mac? Are you sure you'll be warm enough?' She followed Isabel out of the kitchen.

Heledd hovered for a moment. It did not seem right to leave the table cluttered with dirty mugs and glasses and cereal bowls. At Craig Wen she always did the washing up while her father walked to the bottom of the lane to collect the post.

It was odd not to have any morning tasks to do. Saturdays at Craig Wen were always busy, winter and summer, not just with farm tasks but with her father's poetry readings and political meetings. And there were always visitors, neighbours and friends and supporters and other writers and journalists. Heledd would be making tea all day, sometimes.

There would be plenty to do when she went to Craig Wen at half term. Fires to light, damp rugs and quilts to air, windows to clean. I must make a list, she thought.

As she made for the door David looked up and said, 'Heledd, I've got to pop into Jesus this morning. Why don't you come with me?'

Despite weeks of living in Oxford it still disconcerted Heledd, brought up on Sunday School and Bible stories, to hear talk of Jesus and then realise it was Jesus College that was being referred to.

She had visited her father's old college only once before. Her mother had taken her during the Christmas holidays, not long after her father had died. She remembered a stone gateway through which she could see a large square lawn. A man in a dirty black academic gown had crossed the lawn towards them crying, 'Rhiannon! I am so sorry! So sorry! We must arrange a memorial service!'

'Do come,' coaxed David as she hesitated. 'I'll show you the dragons in the dining hall. Your dad used to get his leg pulled about them something terrible. I believe he even wrote a poem about them.'

'He did,' said Rhiannon, coming back into the kitchen and snatching up a bunch of keys from the dresser. '*Dreigiau Iesu* – The Dragons of Jesus. It made him very unpopular because he talked a lot about them being toothless and everyone thought he was getting at the dons.'

'Well, he was,' said David.

Heledd found herself smiling her fixed smile, to hide the confusion she always felt when Rhiannon and David talked about her father with such affection, as though he were their brother instead of the man they had betrayed.

David took Heledd's smile to signify assent. 'Good. Now why don't you make us some more toast? It's Saturday morning and I'm blowed if I'm going to rush.'

Heledd did not reply. She really ought to be thinking about Craig Wen and making her list. But she quite liked the idea of seeing the dragons her father had written a poem about. Perhaps she could do the list tomorrow when she had finished her homework. She mustn't forget it, though; half term was only two weeks away.

6

'Get your wellies on, Heledd, and we'll walk into town,' said David an hour later. 'Pointless taking the car on a Saturday. How Inspector Morse ever manages to park his car in the middle of Oxford I'll never know.'

As they plodded through the slush past the house with the T. E. Lawrence plaque he said, 'Did you see that portrait of Lawrence when your Mum took you to Jesus before? Your father was fascinated by Lawrence of Arabia. He made a real cult of him. Midnight swims in the Cherwell, Arab head cloths, you name it. My word, he used to get some stick about it. Not that he cared.' David's face wore a reminiscent grin. 'What a character! The rest of his year were a dull shower in comparison. Except your mother, of course.'

Heledd said nothing. Stories which implied that her father had had fun at Oxford made no sense to her. He had been an exile there, like she was now. She did not want to think of him dressing up in Arab head cloths, such as were occasionally worn, very much against the rules, by a clique of sixth form boys at her new school.

She tried to remember what her father had told her about Lawrence of Arabia. He had led an Arab revolt against the Turks in the First World War, inspired by stories of chivalrous knights in the Middle Ages. He had exchanged his British Army uniform for Arab robes to express his love of the Arabs and his commitment to the cause of their freedom. He was a brave warrior and an inspired leader of men. 'He became a hero,' her father would say. 'If he'd lived eight hundred years ago we'd be reading about him now in the Mabinogion.' Sometimes he would add, 'Perhaps what Wales needs today is a Lawrence of Arabia.'

So it seemed inevitable that her father's last poem, the poem only she knew about and kept folded up in his last letter, began with a quotation from a poem by Lawrence himself. But Rheinallt's poem was strange and difficult, full of references to truth and lies, myth and illusion, self-denial and destiny. Even the title was disturbing: *Traed Tywod*: 'Feet of Sand'. There was nothing in it about heroes, at least not in any way Heledd could make sense of. But he had been ill, dying, in constant pain, when he wrote the poem. This must be why he had written *I Rhiannon* – 'For Rhiannon' at the beginning of the poem and not *I Heledd*.

Because her father had meant the poem for her; he had sent it to her in his last letter, not to Rhiannon. But it did not seem to be the call to action, the symbolic handing over of the torch, that she had expected. Which was puzzling, because what was the point of her existing, if it were not to carry on her father's work?

There were road works in the Woodstock Road, adding to the terrific congestion of buses, cars and vans as they walked past the Radcliffe Infirmary towards St. Giles. Young people on bicycles took short-cuts along the busy pavements. Several of them shouted greetings at David as they whizzed past.

'Idiots,' said David. 'They'll knock someone over if they don't watch out. Look, that's the Eagle and Child – the pub where we're meeting for lunch. C. S. Lewis's local – we knew you'd want to see it. You like the Narnia stories, don't you?'

Heledd nodded.

'They call it the Bird and Baby.'

Heledd made herself giggle politely.

'With luck it won't be packed with tourists at this time of year. Quick, let's cross the road before the lights change. Do you know about the Martyrs' Memorial? And that's Balliol College over there.'

They crossed the road with a crowd of other people. At the foot of the monument called the Martyrs' Memorial a grimy old woman with a tattered sleeping bag draped round her shoulders sat on a low folding stool. A withered hat containing a few coins lay upturned on the pavement by her feet. The old woman fixed rheumy eyes on Heledd and mouthed something. Heledd blushed with shame for not having any money to put in the hat, but David was already feeling in his pocket. He tossed a couple of pound coins down, then hustled Heledd away as the old woman said, 'God bless you, Professor,' and scooped the money up.

'Homeless, poor old thing,' David said to Heledd over his shoulder. 'It's one of Oxford's biggest problems. That and drugs.' He sounded quite matter of fact. Glancing back at Heledd's shocked face he said, 'I don't suppose you see many beggars in your part of Wales.'

Heledd shook her head. She had heard about the homeless, of course, but she had never seen anyone begging on the streets before.

Homeless! What did it mean? Where did the old lady go at night? Where did she eat her meals? Where was her family?

'Come on, Heledd,' called David, striding out. 'We'd better not get separated. Oxford is murder on Saturdays. Look, there's the Bodleian. No, we go this way.' He seemed to have forgotten about the homeless old woman already.

He led the way across a broad street with cars parked down the middle, and along a narrow lane with high, dark stone buildings on either side. The buildings had windows you could not see into and vast gateways with oak doors, each with a second smaller door let into it through which people sidled in and out. The street had an ancient, secret feel to it, like a medieval town. There was even a group of students, gaudily dressed in tattered velvet doublets like medieval strolling players, reeling about in the middle of the road pushing and shouting at one another.

It took Heledd a few moments to notice that the language they were arguing in was Welsh.

'Oh God,' said David. 'Not again.'

'Don't let him fall over!' the students were shouting at each other. 'Don't let the porters see him!'

'What the hell's going on here?' roared David.

The students leapt into the air as though a machine gun had been turned on them. The youth they had been trying to hold upright, who seemed barely conscious, toppled into the gutter.

'Oh, God, Doctor Middleton, you've got to help us!' cried one of the girls in English. 'If he gets hauled up in front of the procs again he'll be sent down.'

'Tristan Vaughan, don't tell me,' said David, looking down and prodding the boy's buttock with his toe.

'He wasn't with us,' said one of the male students. 'We found him, we did.'

'He's not drunk,' said someone else. 'He –'

'Stoned, I suppose,' said David, giving the boy another prod.

'Starved, more like,' said another boy. 'He does it on purpose.'

'God,' said David. 'An anorexic male. That's all we need. Pick him up and hold him there,' he ordered. 'We'll go in and divert the porters. You've got about ninety seconds, I'd say. Come on, Heledd.'

As he spoke the boy on the ground rolled over and opened his eyes. 'Heledd!' he said. 'Heledd!' He grinned up at her, revealing scummy yellow teeth. '*Stafell Gynddylan ys tywyll heno* – Cynddylan's court is dark tonight –'

'*Heb dân, heb wely*,' whispered Heledd. 'No fire, no bed.' This was her poem, although it was a thousand years old. It was about her, and what she had done.

'Yeah,' said the boy. 'Ain't that the truth. *Stafell Gynddylan* –' He heaved himself onto his knees, swung his arm forward and bent over it in a mocking bow. Before he could speak again he overbalanced, and the others caught him and hauled him to his feet.

'Quick, Tris, Doctor Dave's going to distract the porters –'

'How does it go?' said the boy, pushing his friends away and holding himself upright by clinging to Heledd's shoulder. '*Heb dân, heb gannwyll* – no fire, no candle –' His mouth opened in a soundless laugh and she smelled his sour breath.

'For God's sake,' said David. 'What's he on about?' He turned to one of the girls. 'Take Heledd to sit in the dining hall, will you, Eiry? Don't let this fool give her any hassle. I won't be a minute.'

'Oh, God, thank you, Doctor Middleton!' said the girl called Eiry. 'Quick,' she said to Heledd. They were through the college entrance and across the wet, snow-patched lawn in a second. Heledd looked over her shoulder to see Tristan Vaughan being hustled out of sight under a dark archway.

'Phew!' said Eiry. 'God! If it was anyone else –' she broke off, and turned to Heledd. '*Ti'n Gymraes, on'd wyt?*' she asked. 'You're Welsh, aren't you?'

Heledd nodded. Her head was spinning.

'How do you come to be with David Middleton?' Then Eiry stopped, so suddenly that Heledd collided with her. 'Don't tell me! *Merch Rhiannon!* Rhiannon's daughter!'

Heledd nodded.

'Golly!' said Eiry. 'So your father – your father was Rheinallt!'

Heledd nodded fervently.

'Oh! What a man!' said Eiry. 'Rheinallt is my very top hero. We were with him in those Ministry of Defence sit-ins, all of us in my Welsh group at school, I'll never forget it. He was so incredibly brave, and they were telling these terrible lies about him. And all the time he was so ill and he never told anyone – oh! what a man! And his poetry, it's so passionate! That one about walking away from the gates of heaven, I cry every time I read it. You must have been devastated when he died.'

Heledd nodded. She tried to speak, but Eiry was still in full flood.

'And now here you are with Rhiannon and Doctor Dave,' she said. 'Oh wow, isn't it just the most incredible story? Talk about star-crossed lovers! But poor, poor Rheinallt. And you're the *daughter*.'

Eiry pushed open another oak door and waited for Heledd to go through before hurrying away. As the door swung shut Heledd looked around, smitten once again by the sensation of having stepped back in time. The dining hall was a lofty room with tall windows set in oak panelling, which was hung with portraits in heavy gilt frames. Queen Elizabeth the First gazed disdainfully from the far wall, and there was Lawrence of Arabia in his Arab robes.

The room was furnished with long refectory tables and benches. Heledd ran her hands across the polished oak, breathing deeply. The room exuded the most extraordinary scent, as though the oak of the walls and the furniture had been marinated in food and wine and tobacco and beeswax polish for centuries.

Dad ate here, she thought. He sat at these tables. He smelled this smell. She looked around her and saw the dragons, carved long and slender over the door lintel, spear-headed tails linked together to make a frieze.

Mr Jones of Jesus, he used to say with a sad laugh.

Heledd could not make it out at all. What had Eiry meant about star-crossed lovers?

Heledd thought she knew everything about her father. She thought he had told her everything. He and her mother had met at Oxford, and married two years later while Rheinallt was doing research at Bangor University.

During Heledd's early childhood he had been a lecturer at Bangor, but later he had given up this job to become a full time poet and language activist. That was when her mother had left. She had finished her music thesis but had failed to get work in north Wales. Eventually she had taken up the offer of a junior fellowship at her old Oxford college. 'Only term-times,' she had said. 'I'll be back for the vacations, and lots of weekends.' Heledd remembered her father seeming happy enough with this arrangement, and happy for Heledd to continue living with him so that her life and education should not be disrupted.

Heledd could never quite remember what happened next. It was as though her memory went fuzzy round the edges for a number of years, during which her mother's homecomings became less and less frequent.

We didn't miss her, thought Heledd, trying to think clearly. There was too much else going on. Meetings, campaigns, debates with her father's colleagues, interviews with journalists, and later with the police. Then her father would shut himself away for weeks, finishing a new play or a collection of poems. Or they would be snowed in during the winter. If her mother did make a visit it would take them both by surprise.

At some point Heledd supposed that her mother must have told her that she had fallen in love with another man, but she could not remember a specific occasion. Her worst memory was that of her father saying, 'I suppose it had to happen sooner or later.' That was the only time she had wept. She had wept for her father's heartbreak more than her own, for it seemed then that her mother had always been a stranger to her.

'I'll always be your mother, Heledd,' Rhiannon had said as she waited for the taxi to arrive to take her to Bangor station. 'Nothing can change that.'

But Heledd had shaken her head, and stepped back when her mother tried to kiss her goodbye.

Then came the bad time, the unbearable time. All the terrible things that had happened, that she never wanted to think about again. Her mother married to David Middleton. Her father in prison, in hospital, in prison again. The terrible months during which she had lived with her Aunt Sioned in Maeshafren, unable to see her father, unable to do anything to help him. And then his death.

But how had it all come about? What had happened first? And why did Eiry seem to know all about it?

'Here, you, you shouldn't be in here!'

Heledd looked up to see two stern-faced ladies in overalls, with tea towels over their arms, coming towards her.

'The College isn't open to the public in the mornings!'

'It's all right, Pam, she's with me,' said David, coming into the room immediately behind them. 'Sorry I was so long, Heledd, I was reading my e-mail.'

'Oh, Doctor Middleton,' said the lady called Pam. 'I'm sorry, I'm sure – we're just going to start lunch.'

'We'll get out of your way, then. Come and see the chapel, Heledd.'

Heledd had been so deeply immersed in her thoughts that for a moment she had the impression that it was her father who had come into the dining hall and not David. She gripped the edge of the bench on which she was sitting, and took a deep breath so that she would not begin to weep.

As she looked up, the blue eyes of Lawrence of Arabia seemed to meet hers sympathetically from his portrait.

'Come on,' said David kindly, taking her elbow and steering her towards the door. 'What do you think of the dragons? Good, eh?'

In the college chapel someone was playing Bach fugues very softly on the organ. Heledd heard David sigh. 'You must come to one of your mother's lunchtime recitals. It's lovely sitting here in this space and peacefulness listening to the organ; you forget you're in the middle of a big city.'

Heledd thought of the homeless old woman sitting in the slush at the foot of the Martyrs' Memorial, the traffic roaring around her.

'You can stay here if you like,' said David. 'I daresay the organ reminds you of your Dad, doesn't it? He used to play this one as well.'

Heledd had been told this by her mother, but she could not imagine it. She had only ever heard her father play hymn tunes on the wheezy old chapel harmonium.

David was grinning at her. 'How does it feel to be at your father's old college? Pretty amazing, yes?'

Heledd opened her mouth, then closed it again. She could not begin to express what she was feeling. Her father had had a life here in Oxford that she knew nothing about. Things had happened to him that other people, even ordinary students like Eiry, knew about but she did not.

I used to be inside, she thought with a shiver, and now I'm outside. No fire, no bed.

7

'Oh, what a nuisance, it's packed,' said Rhiannon, going through the narrow entrance of the Eagle and Child and peering into one of the tiny panelled snuggeries into which the old pub was partitioned.

'We could try the café at the Ashmolean,' suggested David.

Isabel and Victoria groaned. Justin and the two other boys who had arrived with Victoria looked on.

'Your mother is so beautiful,' said one of the boys to Heledd.

'David – bring your mob in here – we'll move out the back,' someone was shouting, but Heledd was so startled by the boy's remark that she hardly noticed the scramble which now took place as they took over the corner David's colleagues had vacated for them.

'Thanks, Charlie,' she heard her mother say.

'It's a pleasure, Rhiannon,' replied this Charlie, giving her mother a hug. 'Anything for my favourite bird and her babies.'

'I was going to buy you a drink,' David told him, 'but I've just changed my mind.'

'Pay no attention,' said Rhiannon, catching Heledd's eye. A smile curled up one corner of her mouth. 'Now let's see. Sandwiches.'

'We'll get our own,' said one of the boys. 'Doctor Jones, truly.'

Despite being married to David Middleton Rhiannon still went by the name of Jones, which had been her maiden name as well as Rheinallt's surname. Heledd felt this was cheating, without being quite clear as to why.

After all, she had vowed that her own name would always be Jones, whoever she got married to. Heledd Rheinallt Jones. And all her children would have Rheinallt as one of their names, in honour of her father.

Not that she ever intended to get married.

'Are you sixteen yet?' Isabel asked Heledd, as they squeezed up to make room for everyone. She spoke rather aggressively, as though she had been told to talk to Heledd and didn't really want to.

'Not until *Gorffennaf* – July,' Heledd translated hastily.

'Oh.' Isabel fell silent. Then she said, 'You're a Cancer then. I'm Taurus. I'm fourteen in May. We shouldn't be here, really. There's a notice on the door, no children. But I look older than fourteen, don't I?'

Heledd nodded politely. She studied her mother, who was reading aloud the choice of sandwiches from the menu card. Her thick curly hair was falling out of its loose bun and she was pulling out combs and hairpins with her free hand. Her hair was quite different in colour and texture from that of Heledd, who had inherited her father's fluffy silvery blonde hair. Rhiannon's was tawny, with a bronze, almost greenish gleam. Her eyebrows and lashes were dark whereas Heledd's were so light they were hardly visible. Rhiannon's eyes were a clear hazel, whereas Heledd's, when she regarded herself in the bathroom mirror, were like pale, grey-blue marbles.

Rhiannon was laughing at something one of the boys had said. She relaxed back in her seat and began to pin up her hair again. Justin leaned forward to lift up a lock of hair she had missed from the shoulder of her blue sweater, and handed it to her.

What was there about her mother that made him want

to do that? Heledd was not jealous, merely puzzled. How could you tell if someone was beautiful? It surely had to be more than fair hair and dark eyelashes. Was Victoria beautiful for example? Or Isabel?

She looked at them reluctantly. They both had nice hair, at any rate. Victoria's was dark brown and shiny, falling loose and straight to below her shoulder blades. Isabel's was lighter brown, curlier and wilder. She had tied it back with an elastic band today, to fit under her riding helmet, and it looked as though it wanted to burst free. Both girls were tall and slender, and had light brown eyes and clear skin and pouting mouths to which they applied lipstick several times a day. They both looked older and more sophisticated than Heledd. Yes, they were pretty enough, but they weren't beautiful. Yet Rhiannon was beautiful. Heledd could see it, now she came to look properly. But she could not describe the difference to herself.

I should be more observant, she thought. I am a painter.

She banished the thought at once. She had vowed to give up painting. You had to look at more than people's appearance when you were painting, and she did not want to do that at the moment. Surfaces were all she could manage.

Odd, though, how when it came to painting, the boys had better faces than the girls. More varied. Justin's was bony and acne-scarred, and he wore his curly brown hair in a shoulder-length bob like a young man in a Renaissance portrait. The other two sixth-formers were clearly brothers. They were both tall and fair, and seemed deliberately to be dressed alike in chunky sweaters and baggy green combat trousers. They wore their hair short, with old-fashioned side partings and forelocks falling over their brows.

One of the boys noticed Heledd's scrutiny. He grinned across the table at her. 'The thing to remember,' he said, 'is that I'm Richard, the handsome one, and he's Roger, the ugly one.'

'Or vice versa,' said Roger. Roger was the one who had commented on Rhiannon's beauty. 'But otherwise, we're twins. I'm the elder by forty minutes.'

'But not wiser or more intelligent,' said Richard.

'He wishes!' said Roger.

'She doesn't recognise you without the Arab headgear,' said Justin.

'Don't tell me that's back in fashion again,' said David, pushing through the throng of customers with a tray of glasses and sandwhiches. 'What on earth do your Egyptian and Arab students make of it?'

'It's only him,' said Roger. 'Not me. I think it's stupid.'

'They're rather intrigued, actually,' said Richard. 'We have some very interesting conversations. However, they do offer to beat me up from time to time, I'm happy to say.'

'Honestly, your school,' said David to Victoria and Isabel. 'Talk about more style than substance.'

'Goodness me, Doctor Middleton,' said Richard. 'That is the whole point. So long as we have the style, who cares about the substance?'

'Shut up, Rich,' said Victoria. 'Stop talking so camp.'

'Hear hear,' said Rhiannon. 'Have a sandwich.'

Heledd thought suddenly, I wish Barbara were here.

She'd know how to talk to these people. She'd know what they were on about. I wish we could change places.

Except that that would mean living with Aunt Sioned again.

'Wake up. Heledd,' said David. 'Have a sandwich.'

'She's always like this,' Heledd heard Victoria say to Roger. 'Miles away. In her head, she's still living on a Welsh mountain top.'

'Is she the one who –'

Victoria nudged him to shut up. Heledd bit into her sandwich, taking care not to look up at anyone.

She could hear David at the other end of the table, telling Rhiannon about Tristan. 'Bloody idiot, he's wrecking everything for himself. If the Principal hears about this he'll be in dead trouble. I'm glad he's not one of mine. Supposed to be brilliant, of course. They're always the ones.'

'Do I know him?' asked Rhiannon. 'What's he reading?'

'I'm not sure. Modern languages? Not Welsh, as you might expect, at least I don't think so. Whatever, it wasn't stopping him spouting Welsh poetry all over the Turl this morning. Rheinallt would have been proud of him. What was that he was quoting at you, Heledd?'

Heledd blushed at being addressed directly, but made herself whisper, *'Stafell Gynddylan ys tywyll heno, heb dân, heb wely –'*

'Ah!' said Rhiannon, smiling across at Heledd. '*The Song of Heledd!* She was a Celtic princess,' she explained to the others.

'Oh, do say it so that we can all hear it,' said Richard. 'It sounds so beautiful.'

Heledd regarded him uncertainly, in case he was mocking her.

'Leave her alone, Rich,' said Roger. 'It's not fair, in a crowd like this. We're gawping at her like something in a museum. Mind you, I like museums,' he added to David. 'I'm thinking of doing anthropology. I love the Pitt-Rivers.'

'All the totem poles,' said Richard, nudging Victoria suggestively.

'All the shrunken heads,' said Victoria. 'All hanging up by their hair. Ugh!'

They all laughed loudly. Heledd thought, they weren't really interested in my poem at all. She had been preparing to force herself to stand up and recite it, as she had done in many an eisteddfod. She was glad she hadn't, now.

An hour later they all pushed their way out of the pub and huddled in a group on the pavement, turning their collars up against the drizzle.

'You haven't been to the Pitt-Rivers Museum yet, have you, Heledd?' said her mother. 'It's the anthropological museum. It's the most wonderful hotch-potch of things from all over the world.'

Victoria and Isabel began to sigh, and look longingly towards Cornmarket and the shops.

'I know Heledd will enjoy it,' said Rhiannon firmly. 'But you lot don't have to come. I thought we could go there now for half an hour,' she told Heledd.

'Oh, can't we come too, Doctor Jones?' begged Richard. 'I haven't been for ages, and neither has Rog.' He pronounced Rog to rhyme with Dog. 'And I bet Justin's never set foot in the place. It would do him so much good.'

'Yes I have,' said Justin. 'We went with school once.'

'Infant school.'

'Well, I wouldn't mind seeing a shrunken head,' said Justin.

'Oh come on,' said Victoria. 'I thought you wanted to go to Gap.'

'Gap, dearest Vix,' said Richard, 'will always be with us, whereas an afternoon at the court of Queen Rhiannon is a rare privilege, at least for us humble knights. Doctor Jones – may we?'

'Yuk,' said Isabel to Heledd. 'I can't stand that Richard Clare. I'm sure he's gay.'

'I've got to pop into the Bodleian,' said David, breaking off from a conversation he had been having with another colleague who happened to be passing, laden with bookshop carrier bags. 'I'll leave you lot to it.'

'Coward,' said Rhiannon.

'Well, you clearly don't need me, with all these handsome swains to attend you.' He kissed her, and laughed as she punched him lightly in the ribs.

'Come on, darling,' said Rhiannon, slipping her arm around Heledd's shoulder. 'The rest of you may follow behind, if you wish,' she said to Richard. 'But no silliness, please.'

She might have been admonishing a ten-year-old. Richard bowed with a flourish. The others groaned.

As they crossed the road to the Martyrs' Memorial Heledd saw the homeless old woman still sitting on her stool at its foot. None of them, not even Rhiannon, looked at her or put any money into the upturned hat. They hardly seemed to notice her. Heledd looked away guiltily. As soon as she had some money she would come and give it to this poor lady. She must be freezing, and wet through by now.

The incomprehensible conversation of her companions drifted over her as she thought about the old woman. For some reason she reminded Heledd of Tristan Vaughan lying in the gutter. The wreck of her life was written in her face, as it was in his. They were both outsiders, both regarded as an embarrassment by the rest of the world.

Like me, she thought. And like Dad. He was an embarrassment to a lot of people, including Mam in the end. And so am I.

She felt strengthened by this thought.

8

'Well?' said her mother, some hours later, as she and Heledd hurried home through the rain. 'Good, don't you think?'

Heledd nodded. She made herself say, 'Yes, it was very good,' but in truth the museum had overwhelmed her and she did not know what she felt about it. It was like a Welsh Folk Museum for all the lost people in the world. Thousands upon thousands of artefacts in glass cases were crammed into an enormous, dark building with iron galleries all around the walls reaching up to the roof. Everywhere you looked were baskets, pottery, weapons, jewellery, musical instruments, mourning cloaks and other ceremonial garments elaborately woven from straw and shells and feathers. Canoes and boats had been rigged to hang in the roof space, and a huge carved totem pole towered dominantly over all.

She had been pleased when Victoria, Isabel and the boys had got bored and left. Their crude jokes and facetious remarks had seemed insulting to the people who had made all these extraordinary things. It seemed terrible that objects which had once been essential, even sacred to a way of life, lovingly made and used and cared for, should end up in glass cases being laughed at. It even seemed wrong to gaze and admire as she and her mother had done. As though they were intruding on something private. Something that had been stolen.

And yet – she wanted to go back to the Pitt-Rivers. She felt she would have got on better with the people who had created all the beautiful things it contained, than the clever, materialistic Oxford people she now lived with.

David had arrived home ahead of Heledd and her mother and was lying on the living room sofa watching the sports news on television when they came in.

'Sioned phoned,' he announced, as Rhiannon leaned over the back of the sofa to give him a kiss.

'Oh, God, that woman,' said Rhiannon. 'I only got her letter this morning. Damn. I'd better call her, I suppose. Heledd *fach,* do me a favour and put the kettle on.' She picked up the telephone from the top of a pile of magazines and began dialling. 'Don't worry,' she added to Heledd, seeing her hesitate by the door. 'It's only a silly idea she's got into her head. Nothing for you to worry about.'

She had switched to speaking in Welsh despite David's

presence in the room. He never seemed to mind this, unlike his daughters, but Heledd supposed he must be more used to it than they were. Perhaps he even understood it a bit, having known both Rheinallt and Rhiannon for so many years.

Heledd hovered by the door, waiting for her aunt to answer the phone. At last her mother said, 'Hello, Sioned? Thank you for your letter – no, we've just got in – it's raining – I was going to phone you over the weekend – I must say I'm not at all happy about this. Did you not tell them that it must be Heledd's decision? What? Yes, I know it's more than two years yet but – well if the roof is leaking we'll get it repaired. No, I don't think we should make any exceptions for the bloody Arts Council! No – all right, sorry – but really – yes, I'm aware of that, but that doesn't mean we should do anything she doesn't want us to. You know Rheinallt made it quite clear in his will that no decisions should be made before Heledd's eighteen. He wanted her – all right, Sioned. Look, I'll write to you, and I'll write to them too. Who did you say contacted you? Griff who? – look, Sioned, you're letting yourself be pressurised – it doesn't *matter* what anyone else thinks. Look, I'll write, okay? Yes, all right. Goodbye.'

She pushed in the aerial of the telephone with a thump and threw it onto the sofa. Heledd went quickly into the kitchen, filled the kettle and switched it on. Back in the sitting room her mother was throwing off her coat, scarf and gloves and swearing hard in English.

'What the hell's up?' asked David.

'I haven't had the chance to tell you,' said Rhiannon. 'Nor you, Heledd. Take off your coat and come and sit down for a minute. There's nothing for you to worry about, I promise. Sioned's getting into a panic, that's all. Well, it'd suit her, of course.'

'What would suit her? Calm down, sweetheart, and let's have the whole story.'

'A guy called Griff Jenkins from the Arts Council is trying to get up a campaign to buy Craig Wen to preserve it as a memorial to Rheinallt, turn it into some sort of poet's retreat. He thinks it's an especially good idea because of Rheinallt being buried at Capel Horeb. He's written to Sioned and apparently she's had letters from other people too. Of course they're not contacting *me*, the adulterous wife, not that that surprises me in the least. But they haven't contacted Heledd, either, and it's her house. You haven't had any letters about this, have you, Heledd?'

Heledd shook her head.

'Sioned said Rheinallt wouldn't mind, she says the place was always crowded with poets when he was alive so what's the difference when he's dead? And we should be honoured and all that. Honoured! There's a career opportunity been spotted by somebody, you mark my words. The Rheinallt industry! Let's get in quick before his corpse goes cold!'

'Hush, sweetheart,' said David. 'Don't get so wound up. It's a crazy idea anyway. There was hardly any room for Rheinallt and Heledd to sleep at Craig Wen, never mind anyone else.'

'Sorry,' said Rhiannon. 'You're quite right. They'd have to camp in the barn. And there wouldn't be a flush loo, never mind a bathroom, the spring would never stand it. I suppose the idea would be for the poets to live the primitive life like we did. Do some of them good if you ask me. Hell! I could murder Sioned! Heledd, don't look like that. Come and sit down.'

Heledd remained by the door, unable to move. 'We were –' she began, addressing David awkwardly in English, 'we were primitive.'

Rhiannon and David looked puzzled. She thought for a moment, then repeated, 'We were primitive. Like those people in the museum. It would be like hanging us up in a museum. As if we were an ancient tribe. It makes everything dead, and people laugh at it.'

There was a silence. Her mother and stepfather seemed startled at what was, for her, a very long speech.

'And of course, people would want to rubber neck,' said Rhiannon in a suddenly bitter voice. 'Because of the *scandal*. Because of the nice juicy story – I'm glad you didn't think of that first, Heledd.'

'It'd be like Clouds Hill,' said David. 'Lawrence of Arabia's cottage in Dorset. It belongs to the National Trust now, and it's been kept just as it was when he lived there, very spartan.'

'Rheinallt would never go there,' said Rhiannon. 'And he'd look at the blue plaque on the house in Polstead Road but he'd never knock on the door and ask to see that cottage Lawrence's parents built for him in the garden. I could never understand why, but I do now.'

'The trouble is, poets and heroes become public property,' said David. 'You may have to deal with that eventually, Heledd. Your father *is* a hero to many people in Wales.'

'The last thing he'd have wanted,' said Rhiannon. 'But you needn't worry, Heledd, we'll see that Craig Wen isn't turned into a circus.' She turned back to her husband. 'Of course, the trouble with Sioned is that she's been reading too many articles about the house price boom. What she'd really like to do is to sell the place now before the bubble bursts.'

As Rhiannon was speaking, slammed doors and voices in the hall announced the return home of Victoria and Isabel. They went half way upstairs and then came down again at a run.

'Sell the place! Don't tell us! You've put the house on the market!' said Victoria.

'Sell what place?' demanded Isabel.

'Don't get excited,' said David. 'We're talking about Heledd's Dad's cottage.'

'The one where you used to go up a ladder to bed,' said Isabel to Heledd.

'Hang on a minute,' said Victoria. 'Her Dad's dead, right? So who does his cottage belong to now?'

'When Heledd is eighteen it will belong to her,' replied Rhiannon. 'Until then, her Aunt Sioned and I are the trustees of her father's estate. That means we make all the decisions about what happens to it, according to what her father specified in his will.' She emphasised the last few words slowly, and there was a fierce look in her eye as though she knew what would come next.

'Do you mean to tell me,' said Victoria, 'that we've had to squeeze up in this tiny house to make room for *her*, and we can't afford a mortgage to get a bigger house, when all the time she owns a whole house of her own and you're not making her sell it?' Her voice rose to a shout. 'You cannot be serious!'

'Victoria!'

'Well,' said Victoria. 'At least there's one thing. if she gets the house when she's eighteen we've only got two years to wait. Then she can bugger off back to live there and Iz and me can have a bit of peace.' She stamped upstairs shouting, 'If I haven't cleared off myself by then!'

9

'I'm still fuming,' said Victoria to Justin, at break in the Sixth Form common room the following Monday. 'We get landed with this stepsister, right. Be nice to her, her father's just died. This famous poet her father that she loved so much it sounds unnatural to me, and that his wife loved so much she couldn't wait to leave him and come to live with my Dad. Be nice to this kid, and let her have her own bedroom, she needs her space. So we have to manage with half the space. No mention of the fact that she's got plenty of space. She's got a whole houseful of space, in fact, a house of her own worth hundreds of thousands of pounds –'

'I thought it was a little cottage with no bathroom,' said Justin.

'That's not the point,' said Victoria. 'It's historic, it must be worth a fortune. But it's not only that. It's the principle of the thing. I'm fed up with being nice to her when all she does is stare at you like a lunatic and if she talks at all it's in Welsh. When's she going to start being nice to us for a change? What about our space, Iz and me? I think Rhiannon should make her sell that house so we could get somewhere big enough for us all to have our own rooms.'

'And you might condescend to like her, then,' said Richard, strolling by, hugging a laptop computer to his chest.

'Of course I know you boys think Rhiannon can't do any wrong,' said Victoria. 'It's sickening, the way she has you all grovelling.'

'Dear me,' said Richard. 'We are in a paddy today!'

'I thought you liked Rhiannon,' said Justin. 'You preferred her to your own mother, you said.'

'No, I did not. When did I say that?'

'You did, Vix. She sticks up for you to your Dad, you said.'

'Ha! that was before *she* came along. Her real daughter. It's a different kettle of fish now, let me tell you.'

'You want to watch out,' said Richard. 'You'd better not let your rather interesting stepsister see what you feel about her. She might feel inclined to burn your house down as well as your uncle's. And one might not feel inclined to blame her.'

'Well, thanks a lot!' said Victoria. 'Whose side are you on?'

'I,' said Richard, 'am on the side of Truth, Art and Freedom. I despise this bourgeois obsession with property.'

'Yuk,' said Justin. 'Shut up, you great poser.'

'I bet you've got a room of your own,' snapped Victoria as the bell went.

T. E. Lawrence High School was not only the largest school Heledd had ever attended but the noisiest. Its name was its only romantic feature. The concrete-faced buildings were square, with large windows set between flaking panels of terracotta-coloured plaster. Inside, the students seemed to spend a great deal of time pushing and shoving between blocks, up and down stairs and across walkways, shouting at each other as they went. It was exhausting. Heledd was always getting lost, and being ticked off for lateness.

That Monday, however, the uproar at school was nothing to the uproar in her head. Ever since Saturday her mind had been racing. It was like being shut in a room not knowing how to get out. One moment she was weaving stones and rags and shells into a mourning cloak, the next she was planning to catch the train home to make sure that Craig Wen was safe, that the roof had not collapsed and that her aunt had not sold it to the Arts Council.

At lunchtime she sought refuge in the art studio, which was the one classroom in which she felt almost at home, despite her resolutions about never painting again. The room was empty apart from Mrs Freeling, the art teacher, who was cutting up pieces of mounting board with a scalpel. Looking shyly away from Mrs Freeling's welcoming smile Heledd chose one of the illustrated art books from the store room and sat at a bench by the window to look at it. It was a book of Rembrandt portraits she knew well, as her father had once borrowed a copy from the mobile library. But today she turned over the pages without seeing any of the images.

She ought to find someone to live at Craig Wen. It was wrong for the house to be unoccupied while there were homeless people living on the streets. Perhaps that old lady by the Martyrs' Memorial could live in it, except that she'd probably need someone to look after her. I'd look after her, thought Heledd wildly. She could sleep downstairs in the box bed like Dad used to. I bet she wouldn't mind a tin bath in front of the fire.

'Oho!' said a voice, making her jump. 'The Welsh princess!'

Someone was leaning over her shoulder, looking at the Rembrandt portraits.

'Remember me? I'm Richard, the handsome one.'

He was conventionally dressed today, no Arab headdress, just grey trousers and a black sweatshirt with the green TEL logo. His companion, a slender, dark-skinned boy, even handsomer than Richard, was similarly dressed.

'This is Beni Mohammed ibn Khaled,' said Richard. 'Known as Ben. He is from Syria. He is my bosom friend.' He draped his arms across the boy's shoulders and planted a kiss on his ear.

'Rich,' said Ben, briskly pushing away Richard's arm, 'one day you will go too far.' He grinned at Heledd from the darkest brown eyes she had ever seen. 'I'm always happy to meet a princess.'

'We've come to hear the Welsh poem,' said Richard. 'I was telling Ben, he's never heard anything so wonderful, not even in Arabic. It was like a clap of thunder when I heard those first whispered consonants. There's nothing for it, I shall have to become a Celtic scholar.'

'Well, it makes a change from wanting to gallop about on a camel liberating the Middle East,' said Ben.

Heledd managed to say, 'I'm not a princess.' Her voice came out with a croak, as though rusty from lack of use.

'Oh, but I'm afraid you are,' said Richard. 'How can the daughter of Queen Rhiannon be anything but a princess? No wonder Iz and Vix are feeling put out.'

Heledd looked away, hating his mocking tone.

'Shut up, Richard,' said Ben. 'I must apologise for this boorish and politically incorrect person,' he said to Heledd. 'We're intruding. We'll go away.'

The kindness in his voice gave her the courage to shake her head. 'The poem –' She lost her train of thought, then found it again. 'It's called – it's called *The Song of Heledd*. Her brother the King and all her other brothers have been killed in battle and it's her fault –'

'And your parents named you after her! What a burden!' exclaimed Ben.

'Oh no!' Heledd was proud of her historic name. She believed she had been given it for a purpose. It was a heroine's name.

'Please recite it to us,' said Richard. 'We're not taking the piss, Heledd, really.'

Heledd turned from the bench and looked up at the two boys. She wanted to refuse, but felt that to do so would be an act of cowardice. Her father would have wanted her to do it. And Richard, to her great surprise, had pronounced her name correctly. He must have listened to the way her mother said it, and he must have a good ear, because he'd got the double d right, making it sound like the soft, buzzy th in *this*, not the sharp th in *thing* or *thought* which was what most people settled for. If they ever got past just saying Heled or Helen.

She stood up and cleared her throat.

> *'Stafell Gynddylan ys tywyll heno*
> *Heb dân, heb wely.*
> *Wylaf wers, tawaf wedy.*
>
> *Stafell Gynddylan ys tywyll heno,*
> *Heb dân, heb gannwyll –'*

She faltered, blushing at the boys' intent regard and losing the third line of the verse.

'It's so beautiful,' said Richard. 'What does it mean?'

She thought for a moment, then began shyly, 'It says, Prince Cynddylan's court is dark tonight –' she broke off as Victoria and Isabel came into the studio.

'What are you two doing here?' Victoria demanded of Ben and Richard. 'Push off, would you? We want a word with our stepsister.'

'Sounds ominous,' said Richard. 'I think we'll stay.'

'Look, push off. This is important and it's nothing to do with you.'

Mrs Freeling had stopped cutting mounts and was sending pointed coughs and glares in their direction. 'You'd better all leave,' she said. 'Heleth can stay, but the rest of you can go. I hear a bullying note, Victoria, and I don't like it, especially from a sixth former.' She pointed her scalpel at a notice on the wall which read, 'The Art Room is a Stress-Free Zone'.

'We're not bullying her,' said Isabel. 'We want to talk to her about something. It's important.'

'We want to ask her something,' said Victoria. 'A nice, simple, civilised question. She knows what it is.'

'Victoria, I'm warning you,' said Mrs Freeling.

'Of course we could wait until after school until we could get her on her own,' said Victoria. 'But we thought that wouldn't be fair.'

'Anyway we've got orchestra practice,' said Isabel.

'What is all this?' asked Richard. 'You're not still paranoid about this cottage she owns, are you? Don't pay any attention, Princess,' he added to Heledd. 'They're only jealous.'

'Princess!' said Victoria and Isabel together.

'Victoria – Isabel – you heard what I said,' said Mrs Freeling. 'Out, please. And you boys too.'

'You can see how cramped we are,' Victoria said to Heledd. 'Just think how much nicer it would be for all of us if we lived in a bigger house.'

'Ye gods!' said Richard. 'Come off it, Vix. I'm ashamed of you. How would you feel if your Dad had just died and they wanted to take your home away from you as well? Give the poor girl a break.'

'At least our Dad isn't a criminal,' said Isabel. 'He doesn't go round trying to blow people up like her Dad did. I bet you didn't know that, did you? They go on about him being a poet, but they don't tell you he was put in prison because he tried to blow people up! He was a terrorist! And so's she! She tried to burn Uncle Bryan's house down! Everybody knows that!'

'Isabel!'

'Well, it's true!'

'Isabel. Victoria. Please leave the room at once. I've never heard such spite in my life.'

Far away, Heledd could hear Mrs Freeling rebuking Victoria and Isabel. Ben and Richard stood on either side of her like bodyguards but she was only distantly aware of them. She knew she must speak, but the knot in her stomach had risen into her throat and she felt that if she opened her mouth she would either burst into tears or be sick.

At last she managed to whisper, 'It wasn't like that.' But the only person who appeared to hear her was Ben. He touched her elbow and said, 'Of course it wasn't.'

'They said things like that about his father too,' said Richard. 'And they weren't true either.'

'All right, that's enough,' said Mrs Freeling. 'Out, all of you. Heleth, could you put that book away please, the bell will be going any minute.'

Heledd turned obediently and closed the book of Rembrandt drawings. Mrs Freeling waited until the others had left the room before saying, 'Do you need to talk to anyone, Heleth?'

Heledd shook her head. Avoiding Mrs Freeling's eye she made for the door. As she found herself being swept up by the crowds of pupils now thronging the corridors on the way to their classrooms for afternoon registration the third line of the second verse of the poem came back to her.

Namyn Dyw, pwy a'm dyry bwyll? Save God, who will keep me sane?

10

'But what did your father actually do?'

After school, there had been no avoiding Richard and Ben who were now escorting her along Woodstock Road. Richard was carrying her satchel. Heledd could not understand why they were bothering, and she wished they would leave her alone. But she was feeling ashamed for being too cowardly to stand witness for her father. It was time she began to speak out.

'He wasn't a terrorist,' she said. 'He would never kill anybody. He organised demonstrations and he climbed a television mast once, to make a protest. People thought he wouldn't last three hours because of the cold, but he stayed up there for three days. That was before -' Before his cancer had been diagnosed, but she could not bring herself to mention that.

'Good grief!'

'But he would never kill anybody,' repeated Heledd. The injustice of it swept over her all over again. 'He didn't do – what they said – conspire to make bombs.'

'Was he a Welsh Nationalist?'

'Yes, but the important thing was – is – the language. That's what he believed.' She sighed at the prospect of trying to explain why the language was so important. People would so often say 'But what's the *point?'* in exasperated tones, and then go on about Welsh being forced down their throats. Or they would complain that all the good jobs in Wales went to Welsh speakers and if you only spoke English you were discriminated against. Or they would say that languages created barriers between people so the fewer there were, the better. They didn't understand that your language was not just what you spoke, it was part of what you were. That was what her father used to say. It was a line in one of his poems: *cut out my tongue, cut out my soul.* She managed to say it haltingly out loud. '*Dileu fy nhafod, dileu fy enaid.*'

'Oh,' said Richard. 'It does sound a wonderful language. Say some more. Not your Princess Heledd poem. Something else.'

Heledd thought for a moment, then began *'Wele'n sefyll rhwng y myrtwydd,'* one of her favourite hymns by Ann Griffiths, the eighteenth-century farmer's daughter from Montgomeryshire. She recited the first verse softly as they turned into Polstead Road.

'It's about Jesus in the myrtles, in the Bible,' she explained shyly. 'Look at him standing among the myrtles, it says.'

'We had a myrtle hedge in our courtyard in Damascus,' said Ben. 'I can smell it now. And the jasmine, and the Mohammedan roses.' His voice shook a little. 'My mother loved our garden. How could I have forgotten?'

'They can't go back, you see,' explained Richard. 'And their house was bulldozed.'

Heledd looked at Ben, and he smiled at her. 'It's true,' he said. 'I'll never see those myrtles again. Still,' he added briskly, 'never mind.'

'I've never seen a myrtle bush,' said Richard. 'Have I? Do they grow in Britain? Ever seen one, Heledd?'

She shook her head.

'They're sure to have them in the Botanical Gardens,' said Richard. 'We'll go there, in the summer. Ah!'

They were walking past the house with the blue

plaque. 'The great man!' said Richard, bowing at the plaque with a flourish.

'The great fraud, you mean,' said Ben. The two boys grinned at each other as though this were an old, familiar wrangle.

'Uncrowned King of Arabia!'

'Seven Pillars of Claptrap!'

He can't mean it, thought Heledd. he's just teasing Richard. My father would not have admired a fraud.

The words were out before she could stop them.

'My father wrote a poem about Lawrence of Arabia.'

'Really? Oh, we must read it!'

'In Welsh?' asked Ben. She nodded, avoiding his eye, shocked at herself for blurting out her closest secret to a stranger.

'Well, you must make a translation,' said Richard. 'I insist, Heledd. I can't think of anything more wonderful than a poem about the last Crusader Knight written in the language of King Arthur. I don't care what you say, Ben, he's my hero. If he were alive today he'd have been up that television mast with Heledd's Dad.'

'Oh God!' said Ben. 'He's the last Romantic,' he informed Heledd. 'He's looking for a cause to die for.'

'"Die, for none other way can'st live,"' said Richard, pulling at the collar of his sweatshirt to expose his neck and making noose-tightening gestures with his free hand. 'Heledd, we're going to the Road to Damascus for a coffee. Come with us?'

They were approaching the Middletons' front gate. Heledd shook her head.

'You could pop in and tell Rhiannon – oops! Dr Jones, I should say.'

She shook her head again. Part of her wanted to go, despite the danger of giving away more secrets. She wanted to hear more about why Ben and his father could not go back to Syria. She was astonished that he should sound so matter of fact about it. 'Never mind!' he had said. It was as though she herself might have said: 'I shall never see Craig Wen again, but never mind!' It was inconceivable.

Heledd closed the front door behind her and let her satchel slip to the tiled floor of the narrow hall. The staircase rose steeply in front of her. On her left was the door into the small dining room which was used as a study. She could hear her mother inside with one of her music students. Someone was playing passages of a piano sonata, then breaking off to reply to a question from Rhiannon. Heledd sat on the stairs to listen. She had inherited her parents' love of music but not their skill at making it. Her mother had given her both piano and harp lessons when she was small, but she had never progressed beyond being able to play simple hymns and folk tunes.

Victoria and Isabel must be musical, if they played in the school orchestra. So they had something in common with her mother that she did not. Well, she did not mind. Perhaps Isabel and Victoria needed Rhiannon more than she did. They hardly ever saw their real mother; she hadn't even phoned lately, she'd overheard them grumbling about it. Perhaps they were jealous of Heledd. She seemed to be giving everybody an awful lot of trouble and inconvenience, and there was no need for it.

All she wanted was to be left alone until she could go home to Craig Wen.

Even more so, now. It had not occurred to Heledd until that afternoon that she was one of the lucky ones. She was not like Ben and his parents, who would never again smell the myrtle bushes in their Syrian courtyard, or like the Kosovan refugee children in Year Seven, or Maria, the girl in her form whose family had had to leave Pakistan to escape persecution because they were Christians. She was not like those poor people in flooded Mozambique or bombed-out Groszny. When she was eighteen, she could go home. Home, and Wales, and destiny were waiting for her at Craig Wen. Selling it merely to give Victoria and Isabel more space was something she could never do. But that being so, it was only fair that for the next two years she should get in their way as little as possible, and she had an idea about that.

Heledd crept upstairs to her room and changed out of her school uniform. She sat on her bed thinking about her idea until she heard her mother close the door on the music student, then went downstairs.

'Hello, darling!' Her mother was in the kitchen, pouring boiling water into the teapot. 'You've just missed Eiry. She was asking after you.'

I wonder how Tristan is, thought Heledd. I could have asked her.

'Bright girl,' said Rhiannon, passing Heledd a cup of tea. 'She'd be just the person to help you with your Welsh GCSEs. What do you think? It's very convenient – she lives in the Jesus College flats.'

Heledd nodded obediently, then realised she quite

liked the idea. It was important that she keep up with her Welsh, ready for when she returned home, and the extra work would make the time go faster.

'Good idea,' said David at supper. 'I ought to have thought of it myself. She could probably do with a bit of extra cash too.'

'Hm,' said Victoria. 'I notice we can find extra money for coaching the Princess, but not for coaching me. I don't matter, I'm only doing my A Levels.' She lobbed this remark lightly across the table, watching her father and stepmother warily.

'Vix,' said Rhiannon before David could speak. 'I didn't know you were having problems. You should have said. Is it your French? Your teachers seem very happy with your work.'

'It doesn't matter,' said Victoria. 'It's just the principle, that's all. It'd be nice to be asked, now and again.'

'What about me?' demanded Isabel. 'If she's having extra Welsh I want more riding lessons. Once a fortnight is no good.'

Neither of them looked at Heledd, nor had they addressed a remark directly to her since arriving home after their orchestra practice, despite Rhiannon's attempts to make conversation as supper was being prepared.

David took a swig of red wine and banged his glass down aggressively. Before he could speak Heledd summoned her courage and began, 'I don't mind –'

'Oh,' said Isabel. 'You don't mind if I have riding lessons every week – that's big of you!'

'Isabel!' roared David. Rhiannon closed her hand

gently over his fist and said, 'That's not exactly a fair comparison, Iz. More work for Heledd, more fun for you.'

'So what?' said Isabel. 'I think I deserve something for letting her have my bedroom. She's never even said thank you.'

'That's what I –' Heledd tried again.

'It's quite obvious,' said Victoria, 'that niceness doesn't get anybody anywhere. We're nice, and everybody walks all over us. She's dumb and selfish and everybody runs about after her as if she really was a flaming princess.'

'Vix! Iz!' exclaimed Rhiannon.

'Don't mind us,' said Victoria. 'We know we're not as important as her. You're only our stepmother after all.' She stood up and walked out of the room. Isabel looked fearfully at her father, then jumped up and followed.

Heledd remained in her chair, staring at the pasta congealing on her plate.

'Don't,' Rhiannon said to David. 'Don't go after them, darling. Stay here for a minute. Another row won't help. They're missing their own mother, you know. They haven't seen her for ages.'

'They can bloody well go and live with her,' said David. 'I'm sick of them. They're behaving like eight-year-olds. What about you and me, Rhiannon? What about you and me?'

Rhiannon unclenched his fist from his wine glass and held his fingers between the palms of her two hands until they relaxed. David sighed, then leaned towards Rhiannon until their lips met.

Heledd sat, not looking, not daring to move. Presently

she crept away. As she passed the open sitting room door she heard Victoria throw down the telephone angrily.

'Bloody answer machine again,' she said. 'Where the hell is she? I thought she was only going away for the weekend.'

'She must be still at work,' said Isabel. 'It's only seven-thirty.'

'She should have rung about half term,' said Victoria. 'I suppose she's forgotten all about it as per usual.' She jumped to her feet. 'I'm going to send her an e-mail. I'm blowed if I'm going to be stuck here the entire holiday with that streak of misery.'

'The Princess'll want to go off to Wales,' said Isabel. 'To this house she owns. I don't care, I can have my room back for a week.'

'You shouldn't have said that about her father being a terrorist, Iz,' said Victoria. 'He was set up. That was the whole point. Dad explained.'

'I don't care, I hate her,' said Isabel. 'I bet she'll tell on us to Rhiannon as well. I bet she's telling on us right now. Well, I don't care and I wish she was dead as well as her dad.'

Heledd coughed. The two girls whirled round.

'Oh, so you're listening at doors now as well as telling tales,' said Victoria.

'No,' said Heledd. 'I was going to say –'

'Gosh!' said Victoria. 'Six words in English! We are honoured!'

'I was going to say,' repeated Heledd wearily, 'I don't mind sleeping in the loft.'

Victoria and Isabel stared at her.

'I was going to say at supper,' said Heledd, 'But –'

'What loft?' Victoria asked witheringly. 'We haven't got a loft!'

'Yes we have!' shouted Isabel. 'The hot water tank is up there!'

Victoria began to laugh hysterically. 'Oh yes, the hot water tank. Okay, we'll put a camp bed up there for you, Princess, and a rope ladder. Just be careful not to put your foot through the rafters, that's all, and you'd better make a hole in the roof so you can get some air. And you mustn't disturb the bats, they're protected, but of course you won't mind those, you're probably used to them. Oh yes, it'll be fine, I don't know why we didn't think of it before!' She pushed roughly past Heledd, went into the study and slammed the door.

Sick with shame, Heledd turned away and made for the stairs. Behind her she heard Isabel begin to cry as she picked up the telephone and stabbed out her mother's number yet again.

11

The following morning neither Victoria nor Isabel appeared for breakfast. They dashed out of the house at least half an hour earlier than they would normally have done, while Heledd was still sitting at the kitchen table drinking her orange juice.

'God,' said David from behind his newspaper, wincing as the front door slammed. 'All these tantrums are wearing me out. Roll on half term; at least we'll be rid of them for a week.'

'David,' said Rhiannon. 'Not in front of Heledd. It's not fair.'

'I bet you feel the same, don't you, Heledd?' asked David. 'The way they're behaving at the moment, I wouldn't blame you.'

Heledd said nothing. Only yesterday she would have agreed fervently, although she would never have admitted it to either David or her mother. But since last night she had been haunted by the memory of Isabel's tears as she tried to telephone her mother.

'I do wish Emma would phone,' Rhiannon was saying. 'She forgets how much they need her. They'd feel so much happier if they knew what was happening at half term.'

'She'd better not cry off,' said David. 'I think I've earned you to myself for a week.'

'I did rather hope,' said Rhiannon carefully, sitting down beside him and putting her hand on his arm, 'that we could take Heledd to Craig Wen for a couple of days. I could rearrange my Monday seminars so we could make a long weekend of it. She would like to go, David, and the place will need an airing.'

'I don't see why not,' said David. 'Give us all a breather. I can clear that Monday myself as well, I think. I draw the line at sleeping at the cottage, though. We'll book a b and b. What do you say, Heledd?'

Heledd made herself say, 'I don't mind going on my own.'

David laughed. 'What, all alone on that mountain at this time of year? How do you think you'd manage?'

There was no point in reminding him that she and her father had managed winters at Craig Wen for years.

‘Nice of you to offer, though,’ said David. ‘But no, I wouldn’t mind getting out of Oxford for a few days.’

There was nothing for it but to smile, and whisper her thanks. She slid out of her chair and went up to the bathroom to clean her teeth.

‘Don’t worry about Isabel and Victoria,’ said her mother a few moments later as she helped Heledd into her duffel coat. ‘They don’t mean to be cruel. I know we’ll all shake down together in the end. I just wish I could make it easier for all of you. But you don’t mind if I go ahead with the arrangements with Eiry, do you?’

Heledd shook her head.

‘Now, you’ll be okay, won’t you? You know the way to school by now. See you tonight, darling.’

Heledd let her mother kiss her on the cheek, and left the house, making her way slowly through the streets towards the Woodstock Road. By the house with the Lawrence of Arabia plaque she stopped, reminded of his sensitive face and lonely eyes in the portrait in the dining room at Jesus College.

So Lawrence too had had a private retreat, a home to go to, his own Craig Wen. What had David called it? Clouds Hill, that was it. The place her father had refused to visit because he hated the thought of invading someone’s privacy.

It was good to have a little bit of extra knowledge about her father, that she had not had before. A bit of good knowledge, which she could tie in with her own memories of him refusing to allow a television cameraman inside Craig Wen to film her making Welsh cakes on the kitchen range or climbing her ladder to bed in the loft. Not difficult knowledge about the break-up of his marriage and why he refused to blame or condemn Rhiannon or David.

In the distance she heard the rattle of a train, cutting across the traffic noise. She thought, I could get a train now, and go home to Craig Wen. Perhaps it would be better for everyone if I did. If I just went, and wrote a letter explaining. Then Isabel could have her room back – her private retreat that I've taken away from her.

A woman came out of the house with the Lawrence plaque and shot her a curious look as she came down the path and got into a small car which was parked by the kerb. Heledd moved on hurriedly. At the junction with Woodstock Road she looked up and down. The wide road was full of traffic: buses, bicycles, cars, vans, lorries. The pavements were busy with pedestrians, including people wearing the uniform of her new school, some of whom she recognised. To them, however, she seemed invisible.

If I didn't go to school, thought Heledd, nobody would notice. If I got money out of my savings account I could get a train to Bangor and then a taxi and I could be back at Craig Wen before anybody missed me.

Heledd's heart thumped. She had never played truant before. But this wouldn't be playing truant, it would be going home. Going home. She hardly dare say the words to herself. It couldn't be that easy, could it?

She pulled up her hood and fastened the top toggle of her coat to conceal her only identifiable item of clothing, the school tie. Her grey duffel coat, trousers, and black shoes, newly bought for her by her mother at the beginning of term, were plain and anonymous. The only other school-ish thing she was carrying was her leather satchel. She seemed to be the last person on earth to carry her books in one of these rather than a sports bag, but most adults wouldn't notice that, surely.

Heledd looked up and down the Woodstock Road. She looked at her watch. Five minutes to the registration bell. She could still make it if she ran. She did not move. The stream of school-bound people had thinned to a trickle of mainly older students, some of whom were furtively smoking. None of them looked at her, or paid any attention as she took the right turn into Woodstock Road and set off towards the city centre.

The morning was cold but bright and the pavements were dry for a change. Heledd followed the route she remembered taking with David last Saturday morning, past a block of flats with a sign saying 'Jesus College' by the entrance. That must be where Eiry lived. Heledd walked past quickly in case Eiry should choose that moment to appear, but decided that she would not mind going there for her Welsh tutorials.

Except, of course, that if she was going home to Craig Wen there would be no Welsh tutorials with Eiry.

Heledd made herself walk on, past the Radcliffe Infirmary. Students on bicycles swerved round her and through the entrance to Somerville College, greeting each other cheerfully.

I wouldn't mind a bike, thought Heledd, then stopped herself because bikes were no use at all at Craig Wen. But perhaps her father had had a bike when he was at Oxford. If only she could ask him. If only he were there with her, showing her round all his old haunts.

She did not want to be shown around by her mother, although her father's old haunts must have been Rhiannon's as well. David's too, come to that. That was the trouble.

Isn't it just the most incredible story? Eiry had asked. And it had taken place here in Oxford, when they were all students – or at least, when her parents had been students and David had been a lecturer or something – what they called a teaching fellow. But who had been in love with whom? She could not bear to think about it.

As she passed the closed doors of the Eagle and Child she looked across the road to the Martyrs' Memorial but could see no sign of the homeless old woman. Today Heledd had a few pound coins in her purse, which her mother had given her yesterday to cover the week's school expenses. At least if I do see her I won't need to walk past without looking, she thought.

Meanwhile the next thing to do was to find the bank. Quite soon after her arrival in Oxford her mother had taken her to open an account with some of the money left over after her father's debts had been settled. She had even been issued with a debit card with which she could withdraw money when she wanted to.

'There's not much,' her mother had told her, 'and Sioned and I agree that most of it should be put away for you for when you go to college – that's along with the royalties from your father's books, which will come to you now, of course.'

'That'll make you very rich,' she remembered David saying, drily, 'If he earned two hundred pounds a year from his poetry he was doing well.'

'It will probably be more, now he's dead,' Rhiannon

had said sadly. 'Sorry, Heledd, but that's the way of the world, I'm afraid. Whatever, that money will be saved for you until you're eighteen. But in the meantime we thought it would be nice for you to have a little stash for yourself, to do what you like with. It's not much – about a hundred and twenty pounds.'

'A running away account!' David had commented with a grin. Heledd had blushed guiltily.

'David!' her mother had protested.

'Everybody needs a running away account,' said David, unrepentant. 'I know I do.'

He won't care if I do run away home to Craig Wen, thought Heledd, waiting for the traffic lights by the Randolph Hotel to change. One problem gone. She knew the thought to be unfair. David had been pretty kind to her on the whole. He certainly didn't grumble at her the way he grumbled at Victoria and Isabel. I don't blame them for hating me, she thought.

She walked down Cornmarket towards the shopping quarter of Oxford, looking for a branch of the bank where she held her account. She felt reluctant to ask a policeman in case he wanted to know why she was not at school. The streets were busy even at nine-thirty on a Tuesday morning, and she found herself swept round a corner to where a large group of Japanese tourists were congregated by the entrance to a squat stone tower which looked out of place amongst all the shops and offices and banks at this busy junction. A sign informed her that this was Carfax Tower. She was reminded of Barbara Dawes's letter. You were supposed to climb Carfax Tower if you were in Oxford. Had her father done so? Had Rhiannon been with him?

After looking round uncertainly for a few moments she spotted a street map affixed to a nearby wall and went over to study it. Turning round to try to relate the map to her surroundings she saw the homeless old woman from the Martyrs' Memorial shuffling slowly across the road. It was definitely her. Heledd recognised the ragged sleeping bag with bits of foam coming out of the corners. The old lady was still clutching it round her like a cloak. With her free hand she carried a black bin bag which evidently contained a few possessions, because it clunked as she rested it on the ground every few paces.

Heledd felt the pound coins in her pocket. She was about to pursue the old lady when an Australian voice said, 'Excuse me, can you tell me the way to the Ashmolean Museum?'

Heledd jumped. The speaker was a middle-aged lady wearing a raincoat over what looked like several layers of jumpers, and a bright red beret.

'I – I don't know. I'm sorry –' Heledd pointed vaguely at the map.

'Geoff!' shouted the woman. 'There's a street plan over here! Thank you, dear,' she said to Heledd. 'This is our very first visit to Oxford, you see. It's a fine city, isn't it?'

Heledd smiled politely, edging away towards the crossroads. She was in time to see the old woman turning into the entrance to the covered market. She waited for the traffic lights to change, then crossed the road and followed.

The covered market smelled of flowers and cucumbers and freshly hosed-down floors. Heledd passed a greengrocer's with a pyramid of creamy cauliflowers stacked up outside, a butcher's, a shop selling luggage and umbrellas, an antiquarian bookshop and a café with a blackboard outside listing dozens of varieties of coffee.

There was, however, no sign of the old lady. Heledd was ashamed to find herself feeling relieved. She looked round, but could not see the way out.

'All right, darlin'?' boomed a voice close to her ear.

Heledd jumped. The voice belonged to a grinning man in a white apron who was standing by the open door of his cheese shop.

'You look lost!'

'No – no –' Heledd looked wildly round. She wanted to run away, but if she did that he might get suspicious and call the police. She thought fast. 'I was looking for – I was looking for the Bodleian Library –' she blushed, hearing her hissing North Walian accent.

'Oh yeah, no prob, go out by that exit there, that'll bring you out into the Turl, right? Take a left, then cross over and go down Brasenose Lane. You can't miss it after that. Fresher, are you? Welsh, eh? Still getting lost? I'm getting old!' roared the cheese man to his neighbour, who was taking the shutters down from a window full of antique jewellery. 'The students get younger every year!' Heledd heard him laughing loudly as she hurried away in the direction he had indicated.

She recognised the Turl. It was the narrow lane with high buildings on either side, down which David had brought her on Saturday. Today it was whizzing with cyclists in both directions. And there was the entrance to Jesus College.

Heledd thought impulsively, I should just like to have

another look at that portrait of Lawrence of Arabia. Perhaps if I ask –

She was about to step out into the Turl when she saw David pedalling towards her, cycling abreast of another man whose academic gown flapped dangerously round his bicycle wheels. The two men were deep in conversation, oblivious to the other traffic. Heledd dived back into the market and lurked among the stalls until her heart slowed down. Presently she came upon a different exit, and found herself in a wide, busy street surging with traffic. Tall stone buildings rose up on either side, the weak sunshine flashing on their high gable windows.

She wandered along, not knowing whether to turn right or left. Then she saw a painted sign propped outside the carved stone porch of a church. 'St Mary's University Church,' it said. 'Tower Open. Convocation Coffee House.'

The oak doors inside the porch were open, and Heledd went in.

12

The church was huge, dimly empty and full of quietness. The noise of the city faded to a low, surging murmer, like the sound of the sea. Heledd looked cautiously round, then slid into a side pew and sat down with relief.

She knew about churches. She and her father had attended the tiny Horeb chapel a mile's walk from Craig

Wen, but he had taken her to visit many other churches: the Cathedral in Bangor, for example, and the parish church of Aberdaron at the very end of the Llŷn peninsular, where the poet R. S. Thomas had been the priest. In the ancient little church of Abergynolwyn on the slopes of Cader Idris her father had stood at the lectern and read aloud from the Welsh Bible which had been left open upon it. '*Yr Arglwydd yw fy Mugail* – The Lord is my Shepherd . . .' Her father had loved the language of the Bible. It permeated his speech and his writing to such a degree that Heledd could hardly think about her father without thinking of the Bible, and chapel, and Sunday school. Since his death, and her move to Oxford, chapel and Sunday school were lost to her, but many passages from the Bible were engraved upon her soul. Particularly the Psalms, which might have been written by a Welsh shepherd holding a lamb in his arms on a cold hillside. And the bit she particularly loved, from the Book of Zechariah, about the man standing among the myrtles, that Ann Griffiths had turned into her wonderful hymn and that reminded Ben of the home he would never see again.

The man in the myrtles, he was riding a red horse, remembered Heledd dreamily. And he stood among the myrtle trees and behind him there were horses red, and speckled, and white – she loved that bit about the speckled horses, *meirch brithion.* She imagined them wandering about in a kind of scented garden with a stream running through it, and a desert in the background, like the Garden of Eden. It was the kind of scene she would once have painted.

The peacefulness of the church calmed her. She sat for

a while, vaguely trying to remember what she ought to be doing. The bank, she thought. The railway station. What was supposed to happen after that? Ah yes, home to Craig Wen on the next train. Or . . . back to school before she was missed? Silly, perhaps, to think of running away to Craig Wen. She'd only be brought home again, and they'd promised to take her there at half term anyway. She swallowed, trying not to weep. I am a coward, she thought.

Reluctantly she stood up and left the pew. Looking round for the way out she saw a notice saying, 'Tower Open. Admission £1.50.'

If she climbed the tower perhaps she would be able to see where she was, and could find her way back to Woodstock Road without running into David. It was important that she was not caught, because if she were, he would surely think she was avoiding school because of Isabel and Victoria.

An elderly lady wearing a badge saying, 'Friend of St Mary's Church' sold her a ticket to the tower, advising her to be careful as the steps were steep and narrow and there weren't many passing places.

'You're the first today so you should be all right.' She looked curiously at Heledd. 'Are you a student?'

Heledd nodded, smiling evasively. It was not exactly a lie; they were always called students, not pupils, at T. E. Lawrence High School.

'It's the best view of Oxford of all,' said the lady chattily. 'I climbed it many a time when I was a girl.' As Heledd mounted the first few steps to the tower she heard the lady say to someone, 'French. You can tell. Oxford's all language schools these days, it's not what it was.'

Heledd climbed the steep spiral steps to the tower, the rubber soles of her shoes making no sound on the old stone. She kept a cautious hold of the rope balustrade which was fixed to the wall of the stair-well.

It was quite a long climb and she felt quite breathless by the time she stepped out onto a parapet secured by metal railings. She shivered as her hood blew back, and clutched the railings to steady herself. It was windy up here, and cold, but it was high enough to catch the sun, which cast its primrose light across the roofs of the buildings spread out below her.

Heledd edged her way round the parapet, taking in the view over the city. Domes and turrets and spires and towers clustered around her like the instruments in some petrified orchestra. She looked down over the railings, past pairs of carved stone gargoyles, to a patch of bright green lawn which seemed a thousand miles away, yet at the same time near enough to step onto.

She swayed a little, feeling dizzy. She had to fight a sensation of being able to fly. It was as though something were urging her to leap into the air and fly about among the lacy turrets and curvy gables. Like when the Devil took Jesus up to a pinnacle of the Temple in Jerusalem and dared him to cast himself down.

Resisting the impulse, she leaned back as far away from the parapet as she could, pressing against the stone wall of the tower. She was not afraid of heights. She and her father had climbed Snowdon and all the other great peaks near her home, many times. She knew about vertigo but had never experienced it before.

She made herself look again. An empty Coke can had got stuck behind one of the gargoyles, barely three feet from her hand, and she had to fight a wild urge to climb over the railings to retrieve it.

It was frightening, but she wanted to carry on looking. The sun was brighter now. It was as though the city had come alive for her, was showing her its beauty. She thought of Jesus in the Wilderness, being taken up by Satan to a high place and shown all the kingdoms of the world. *Holl deyrnasoedd y byd.* She heard the voice of the Devil: all this can be yours, if you will but worship me. *Hyn oll a roddaf i ti, os syrthi i lawr a'm haddoli i.* She whispered the words to herself in Welsh, moving cautiously round the parapet but still looking out over the city.

'Wicked view, innit,' said a voice. 'Though it kills me to admit it.'

Heledd stood still.

'Hell fire, it's cold!' said the voice.

Heledd did not move. She heard a step, and a long choking cough. Keeping hold of the parapet, she turned her head.

'Iesu!' said Tristan Vaughan. 'It's you! *Stafell Gynddylan* – Well, of all the church towers in all the world –'

Heledd's terror began to ebb.

'No fire, no candle, eh!' said Tristan Vaughan in English. 'Ew, I thought I'd dreamed you! But I heard all about you, after.' He giggled feverishly. He was shivering inside the filthy army greatcoat he was wearing. His feet were sockless in his ancient trainers, and he stank.

'Have they sent you after me?' he asked vaguely. 'What day of the week did you say it was?'

'It's Tuesday,' said Heledd. '*Dydd Mawrth.*'

'I thought they might have sent you after me, I dunno why.' He swayed against the railings as Heledd had done, coughing hoarsely. 'Tell me when it's morning,' he said, sliding down the wall onto his haunches, then slipping sideways until he was lying down on the narrow floor of the parapet.

'It's morning,' said Heledd. 'It's ten o'clock.' She looked at him helplessly. 'Please stand up.'

'Is it ten o'clock?' said Tristan, sitting up and wiping his nose on his sleeve. Heledd heard catarrhal noises in his chest as he breathed. He fumbled in his pocket and pulled out a white plastic tube which he put between his lips, inhaling with a rattle.

'You shouldn't be up here if you've got asthma!' cried Heledd.

'Only place I can breathe, sometimes,' said Tristan, inhaling again. 'What time did you say it was?'

'Ten o'clock!'

'That's all right, then,' said Tristan. He smiled at Heledd. 'Made it.' He began to scramble upright, clinging onto Heledd with one hand and the railings with the other.

'You're ill,' said Heledd desperately. 'You must come down.'

'I'm coming down now in a minute,' said Tristan. 'Did you say it was ten o'clock?' He laughed, and punched the air. 'Ten o'clock, wey hey!'

He swept his arm in a wide arc across the prospect of the city. 'Well, Heledd *ferch* Rheinallt, what do you make of *Rhydychen*?'

Heledd's terror began to subside. She looked uncertainly at Tristan. 'Ox-ford,' he repeated slowly. *Rhyd-ychen.* The ford of the oxen.'

'It was tempting me,' whispered Heledd. 'Like Jesus in the Bible.'

'*Holl deyrnasoedd y byd.*' said Tristan. 'Yeah. What a con. One thing, from up here you can spit at it. Oxford, home of lost causes. Ha! That's bloody true, that is, and here's its very latest lost cause about to throw himself off this f –' he glanced at Heledd and stopped. 'Forget it,' he said. 'I'm okay.'

'I felt like that when I got up here,' said Heledd. 'It's vertigo. It makes you want to. Jump off, I mean.'

'The town as well, believe me.'

'Why did you come here, then?'

'Why did your Dad come here? Or your Mam, for that matter, the blessed Rhiannon?'

'I don't know!' cried Heledd. 'Dad said some of the best things in his life happened to him at Oxford, and some of the worst. But I don't know what he meant. I don't know why he didn't go to a Welsh university.'

'Oh, that bit's easy,' said Tristan. 'Oxford is the place, you see, for the upwardly mobile Welsh. The *crachach.* Always has been. Come to Jesus College, join the Dafydd ap Gwilym society and bingo, a job with BBC Wales and you're made. That's what all good Welsh mams and dads want for their little dears, didn't you know? Oh, the sacrifices they make, and what good does it do them? They still die in the end.'

'Is that why you came?'

'If you really want to know,' said Tristan, 'I came because your Dad came here. The Man on the Mast. Poet, patriot and blinking idiot, if you ask me. What was it all for? A dead language?'

'You're Welsh,' said Heledd. 'You know – you should *know* what it was all for.'

'Yeah, well. I had faith like that once. Dunno what happened to it. Never mind. It's Tuesday, you say? Ten o'clock?' He coughed roughly for several minutes. 'Yeah,' he said dreamily. 'Better eat, I daresay. Do not go gentle into that good whatnot.'

The sound of other visitors climbing to the tower was now heard. 'Come on,' said Tristan to Heledd in Welsh. 'Let's get from here.' He ducked past the Australian lady with the red beret. Heledd followed him down the spiral stairs, past the queue of people buying tickets for the tower and back into the nave of the church.

'This is an awful place,' said Tristan, looking up into the high roof. 'It's where those guys were put on trial, the ones that were burnt at the stake. You heard about them? Latimer and Ridley and the other one – Cramner. That's religion for you, eh? They were Protestant and old Queen Mary was a Catholic. Ring any bells?'

So the church was not a quiet, peaceful place at all. The speckled horses had never grazed in this garden.

'I've seen the Martyrs' Memorial,' said Heledd after a moment. 'There was an old lady –'

'Churches,' said Tristan with a shudder. 'They do my head in.'

'But you were all night on that tower,' said Heledd. 'You must have been. They said I was the first one today, and you were in front of me.'

'Yeah, well,' said Tristan. 'I had to sleep somewhere, didn't I? I'm p.n.g at Jesus at the moment. *Persona non grata,*' he explained, seeing Heledd's mystified look.

'Rusticated. Not wanted in this University at the moment. Can't say I blame them, really.'

'What's rusticated?'

'Sent home,' said Tristan. 'To consider my attitude. What home, they didn't think to ask.'

'What?'

'Forget it,' said Tristan. 'Nothing you need worry about.' He held a door open, then followed her into a busy square, on the far side of which stood the Radcliffe Camera, an elegant circular building whose dome had dominated the view from the top of St Mary's tower.

'Where are we?' cried Heledd, running to catch up with Tristan as he dodged between cyclists and pedestrians across Radcliffe Square.

'Jesus is that way,' said Tristan. 'Don't let your Mam see you with me, she'll go ballistic.'

'She will anyway if she sees me,' said Heledd. 'I'm supposed to be in school. But what do you mean, what home?'

'Forget it,' said Tristan, diving into the covered market.

'Do you need money?' asked Heledd, hurrying after him and nearly falling over a girl and her dog who were begging in the entrance. 'I can lend – I can give you some money.'

Tristan stopped, and turned. 'Heledd *ferch* Rheinallt,' he said, 'you're a good girl. He'd a bin proud of you. I'm sorry I bitched about him. But you don't need to worry about me.' He snatched an apple from a box outside an organic food stall and bit into it, waving cheerfully at the furious face of the girl behind the counter.

'Wait,' said Heledd. She hastened after him, fumbling in the front pocket of her satchel. She pulled the key from its tissue wrapping and held it out to him. 'If you haven't got anywhere to go,' she said, 'you can go to Craig Wen.'

'You don't need to worry about me,' repeated Tristan. He took the key, staring at it. 'Is this the key to your house?'

'Where Dad and I used to live, yes. There's no one there at the moment. You can stay there, if you like.'

'Don't be daft – I don't even know –'

'It's on the mountain road out of Llandegai, about six miles –' As she spoke she saw Tristan's eyes focus again. He looked over her shoulder and muttered, *'Uffern dân*, hell fire, I gotta get from here.' He stuffed the key into the pocket of his greatcoat and stumbled away through the market. Heledd turned to be confronted by the girl from the organic food stall.

'Where is he?' shouted the girl. 'Stealing my apples! He was with you!'

'I'm sorry,' said Heledd. 'I'll pay. He was hungry.' She fumbled in her purse and gave the girl a pound coin.

'Blimey,' said the girl. 'You could have had another for that. But I'll keep the change for my trouble. Is he your boyfriend? Paying for him already! That's bad, that is.'

Heledd took in none of this. What have I done? she thought. Aunt Sioned's got the only other key. What about half term? What am I going to tell Mam?

'You okay?' asked the girl from the organic food stall.

Heledd nodded quickly, edging away. The girl watched her for a moment, then shrugged and went back to her work.

13

'I feel awful,' said Victoria to Justin, as they sat side by side at two computer terminals in the school library on Wednesday afternoon. "I don't mind sleeping in the loft!" she said! And I laughed at her! I didn't mean to. It just came out.'

'I didn't know your house had a loft,' said Justin.

'Of course it doesn't. Only a space in the roof for the hot water tank. We had a burst one winter or I wouldn't even know that.' She swivelled the mouse impatiently on the cover of the script of *Top Girls* which was serving as a mouse pad, and watched the pointer dart about the screen.

'I said to Iz, you've got to admit, she did offer. She must have begun to notice us a bit. But Iz thinks she hates us. She thinks she tells Rhiannon horror stories about us when they talk Welsh together.'

'She doesn't look the spiteful type,' said Justin.

'She must hate us, though, when you think,' said Victoria. 'I mean, we're the English and she's the Welsh.'

'Mm,' said Justin. 'You going to London this weekend?' he asked.

'Mum's coming over on Sunday. She phoned last night, thank goodness,' said Victoria. 'Iz gets so frantic when she doesn't phone. She was away last weekend, she had to go to New York to sort something out, she said. She might have let us know. I mean, what are mobiles for?'

'You'll be okay over half term, then,' said Justin.

'Looks like it. Dad and Rhiannon are taking the Princess off to Wales. I'm going to get myself into one of those workshops at the National Theatre if I can. Iz can have Mum all to herself. I can't wait. You must come over one day.'

Justin said, 'Well, I was thinking of going off with Rog and Rich in the camper. Rich's passed his test as well now.'

Roger's and Richard's eighteenth birthday present from their parents had been a very old Volkswagen camper van which their friends had helped to renovate.

'In the passion waggon?' said Victoria. 'Is that wise?'

'Well, Ben's coming as well, so my virtue's in no danger.'

They both giggled, earning a reproving cough from the librarian.

'Anyway, Richard's not gay,' said Justin. 'He only camps about to wind people up. Ben wouldn't have it, anyway. Moslems are very against it, he told me.'

'But they're always holding hands.'

'Arabs do. When we lived in Bahrain you saw it all the time. And kissing.'

'Blimey! So what's Richard playing at, then?'

'He's pretending to be Lawrence of Arabia. He had the video for Christmas. Anyway, Ben likes your Princess.'

'You're joking!'

'No, I'm not.'

'I don't believe it.'

'It's the mystery. Him and Richard want to find it out.'

'What mystery?' said Victoria scornfully. 'There's no mystery. Her Dad died, that's all.'

'Yeah, but you said yourself, she lives on a different planet. So there must be something.'

'Well, whatever it is, I'm fed up with it,' said Victoria.

'I don't know what's got into you all. First Rhiannon, and now her flaming daughter.'

'If you two aren't using those computers,' the librarian's voice interrupted, 'there are others who need them.' Her last words were drowned by the ringing of the bell for the end of afternoon school.

'Come on,' said Victoria. 'We'd better not leave the Princess in the lurch again, and Iz won't wait unless I do. Ugh! Don't tell me it's sleeting again! I need some new boots; these are falling apart.'

On the way home Isabel said to Heledd, speaking quietly so that Victoria and Justin in front would not hear, 'Did you bunk off school yesterday?'

Heledd was still deep in anxious thought about Tristan and the key to Craig Wen, so she was slow to catch Isabel's question.

'Ben was looking for you all over,' said Isabel. 'I think he fancies you.'

Heledd's face heated up. She shook her head.

'You needn't worry, I won't tell.'

Heledd realised that Isabel was holding out an olive branch.

'You want to be careful. If Dad ever found out he'd go crazy.'

Heledd said, 'Please – please don't say anything to Mam.'

'I wouldn't, I promise, honest.'

'Thank you.'

'Crumbs,' said Isabel, 'I wouldn't dare bunk off. Where did you go?'

'I climbed a tower,' said Heledd, 'And I looked upon the city and on the kingdoms of the world, like Jesus in the Bible, you know.'

An appalled look came over Isabel's face. 'You're really into the Bible, aren't you?' she said. 'Are you a Happy Clappy or something?'

Heledd was silent. She had no idea what Isabel meant.

'You don't have to be offended,' said Isabel crossly. 'I only asked.'

'My father liked to read the Bible,' said Heledd, making an effort.

'Oh, I see,' said Isabel. 'In Welsh, I suppose.'

'Yes, in Welsh, but sometimes in English too.'

'Oh.'

An awkward silence fell between them, which lasted all the way home.

14

Towards the weekend the temperature dropped and the sleet turned to snow. According to the weather forecasters, heavy snow was falling over the whole of Britain, especially over high ground, and drivers were being advised against making unnecessary journeys.

Marooned in Oxford Heledd could not stop herself fretting about Tristan and Craig Wen. Had he gone there? What if he had got lost in the snow on the way? How would he manage? She hadn't had the chance to explain anything to him, like where to get water or how to light the kitchen range or the oil lamp. She couldn't remember if there was any coal or logs, or any gas left in the bottle. What would the Davieses Tanygraig do if they thought someone was trespassing at Craig Wen? Every time the telephone rang she felt sure it must be the North Wales police to say that they'd arrested Tristan for breaking and entering, or worse, found him frozen to death on the cold hearth.

The only practical thing she could think of to do was to write him a letter containing a list of all the things he might need to know, and send it off to him, together with some money in case he needed to buy food. One of the jobs she had done before returning home last Tuesday afternoon had been to find her bank and cash fifty pounds, which was the most her debit card allowed her to draw at any one time. She had put a ten pound note in the homeless old lady's hat, hurrying shyly away before she noticed. After sending another twenty to Tristan there was twenty left. In case of emergencies, she told herself.

The postman will be surprised at having to deliver a letter to a stranger at Craig Wen, she thought. He'll probably think we've rented it out. He's sure to walk up the lane to see who's there, so if Tristan has got any problems he'll be able to help. That is, if the lane isn't blocked with snow.

On Saturday morning when she woke up the snow had stopped falling and the sky was blue above the bare horse chestnut trees.

'What we could all do with,' said David, brewing coffee in the kitchen, 'is a good tramp across Port Meadow.'

'Good idea,' said Rhiannon, sorting through the post. 'Oh, hello, here's something that'll interest you, Heledd.'

She handed a stiff square card across the table. It was white, with green printing on it.

'*The Principal of Jesus College,*' read Heledd, '*requests the pleasure of your company for St. David's Day, in the Harper Room at 4.15p.m. on Monday March 1st.*'

'It's lovely, you'll have to come,' said Rhiannon. 'We have tea, and there's a Welsh service in the chapel, and a formal dinner afterwards. She should come, David, shouldn't she? At least to the tea and the service.'

'Definitely,' said David. 'Rheinallt's daughter – guest of honour at least. You two, as well,' he added to Victoria and Isabel, who were sitting about in their pyjamas. 'Widen your horizons a bit.'

'No culture on a Saturday morning, Dad, please,' groaned Victoria. 'Anyway it'll be all in Welsh.'

'No it won't. Bit of both – English and Welsh. You might get roped in for a recitation, Heledd.'

'David, don't,' said Rhiannon. 'In front of all those old dons. It would be terrifying.'

Heledd was trying to smile, but she was thinking of last year's St. David's Day. Her father had still been quite well, and they had walked down the mountain to buy daffodils in the village, and stopped to drink a cup of tea with the minister. In the evening there had been a *Noson Lawen* at Horeb chapel. Her father had recited a poem to his own harp accompaniment, and afterwards there had been *cawl cennin*, leek soup, and Welsh cakes and bara brith. It wouldn't ever happen again. He was dead now, and buried in the graveyard of that same chapel. He had asked specifically to be buried, not burned. And to have no headstone. Aunt Sioned thought it was morbid and unhealthy, but had not been prepared to say so in front of the minister, so her brother's wishes had been respected.

I must put daffodils on his grave on St. David's Day, thought Heledd. I must get there somehow. She tucked the idea away carefully to think about. It might not be impossible. Twenty pounds would be enough for the train fare, surely. When she had at last found the railway station on Tuesday afternoon she had collected a number of leaflets with timetables, but had not thought to ask about fares.

There was a train passing now, at the bottom of the garden, going north.

'The snow can't be that bad,' remarked David. 'The trains are still running.'

Victoria borrowed Rhiannon's wellingtons and departed for the Road to Damascus. Isabel began to make pointed remarks about how grateful they would be at the stables if she turned up to help clear the snow.

'We don't really want to get the car out today if we don't have to, now do we, Isabel, be sensible. Besides there's plenty of snow-clearing to be done here. Come on, both of you, get your boots on.'

Isabel pouted, but did not argue. As she and Heledd stepped into their wellingtons she said, 'I wish we lived in the country. We could have lots of animals then, not just ponies.'

'We had a pony at Craig Wen,' ventured Heledd. 'And a goat.'

'It's not fair,' said Isabel as they tramped across the snowy garden. 'I've never been allowed a pet, ever. Not even a cat or a rabbit. Mum's allergic.'

'You're a bit old for rabbits now, Iz,' said David over his shoulder.

Isabel's face puckered up sulkily. Heledd wondered why her mother had not noticed that Isabel would have liked a pet. It seemed such a small thing to want.

Despite snow-clearing and a brisk walk after lunch, the day seemed to drag. Indoors, the phone rang incessantly, keeping Heledd's heart in her mouth, but none of the calls came from Wales, not even from Aunt Sioned. To distract herself she pulled her suitcase out from under the bed and took out the envelope containing her father's last poem. She took it downstairs to the sitting room and read it through carefully. She tried to make more sense of it than she had been able to do last time she tried, but with little success. Even the English verse, the one by T. E. Lawrence that her father had written out at the beginnng of his poem, made little sense.

Looking over Heledd's shoulder as she came in with a tray of tea, her mother read the words aloud. *'I loved you, so I drew these tides of men into my hands, and wrote my will across the sky in stars.* Goodness! What have you got there? Sorry, darling,' she added quickly, as Heledd jumped. 'I won't look if you don't want me to.'

'It's only a poem,' said Heledd. 'Dad copied it out.'

'I know that poem off by heart,' said Rhiannon with a sigh. 'Your father was always quoting it.'

'Because it was how he felt about you,' said David.

Rhiannon caught her breath. After a moment she said, 'Rheinallt always felt very close to Lawrence of Arabia. He often talked of writing a long poem about him, but I don't think he ever got round to it.'

Heledd gripped the sheets of manuscript between her fingers. Her father's own verses and the page with the dedication were concealed by the sheet of paper on which he had copied out Lawrence's poem; she might simply have been holding a letter.

'God,' said David. 'What it says about all of us, I don't know, to make a national hero out of such a fantasist and a liar, not to mention –'

'Yes, but,' began Rhiannon, 'for Rheinallt, you know, David, that was half the fascination.'

'I've just had yet another book about Lawrence to review,' said David to Heledd. 'You can read it if you like. It's in the study.'

I don't want to read a book about a fantasist and a liar, thought Heledd. But she knew she would have to.

15

The snow did not prevent Victoria and Isabel's mother, Emma, from coming to see them on Sunday as she had promised. She was civil to Rhiannon, smiled and said 'Hello,' to Heledd in quite a friendly way, but was clearly relieved when Rhiannon announced that she and Heledd had been invited to walk down to the Jesus College flats to visit Eiry and see about Heledd's Welsh tutorials.

Eiry shared a flat with three other girls, all of whom were Welsh speaking. It was very untidy, with clothes and books littered everywhere, and Radio Oxford playing loudly in the kitchen.

'It won't be like this in the week,' Eiry hastened to reassure Rhiannon, handing round mugs of instant coffee. 'We're hardly ever all here together, except at weekends.'

'We thought the best thing to do would be to show you the textbooks Heledd's been using,' said Rhiannon. 'The Welsh syllabus is a bit different from what they're doing at TEL. Don't worry, though, we're not expecting you to take full responsibility for her Welsh medium education.'

They stayed at the flat for quite a while, talking over the possibilities. Heledd sensed that her mother was in no hurry to go home. She invited Eiry to walk down to the Ashmolean Museum with them for lunch. Presently the three of them were making their way along St. Giles. Heledd looked out for the old lady by the Martyrs' Memorial, but it was surrounded by brown heaps of snow thrown off the road.

'That's the Martyrs' Memorial,' said Rhiannon.

Heledd nodded. She could not help saying, 'There's an old lady who sits there usually.'

'It must be terrible to be on the streets in this weather,' said Eiry.

'Awful,' agreed Rhiannon. 'But there's quite a good day centre now, I believe, off the Cowley Road somewhere.'

They aren't a bit bothered really, thought Heledd. At least I gave her ten pounds. Then she felt ashamed. Her father would not have considered it enough.

'I hope Tristan's found somewhere to go,' continued Eiry. 'He worked at the Salvation Army hostel over Christmas, and lived there, but what he's been doing since getting rusticated I don't know. I lent him twenty pounds, but that won't get him very far, will it?'

'What on earth do you mean?' asked Rhiannon. 'Hasn't he gone home? Where is he from?'

'Swansea,' said Eiry. 'He was living with his Nain, but she died last November, and she only had a council flat. I think his mother's dead as well.'

'Good God!' exclaimed Rhiannon. 'Does the College know all this?'

'I don't know,' said Eiry. 'He wouldn't have told them. He said we weren't to worry, he had a key, or something. He's probably squatting somewhere.'

Heledd listened anxiously. Tristan must have seen Eiry after she had given him the key to Craig Wen, and it sounded as though he intended to go there. Had he arrived? Was he safe? What would happen if she turned up at the cottage with her mother and stepfather next weekend and found him there?

His Nain had died at about the same time as her father. So they did have something in common, after all.

She ate a salad sandwich for lunch without tasting it, and gazed at the pictures in the Ashmolean without seeing them. She even forgot to look out for the Mark Gertler still life of apples in a paper bag, or the Pissaro painting of an old farmhouse in the snow which so reminded her of Craig Wen. Rhiannon and Eiry talked over her head, not seeming to notice her preoccupation.

Eventually her mother said, 'You're very quiet, Heledd.' She laughed. 'It must be getting quite unusual, for me to have noticed.'

Heledd said the first thing that came into her head. 'Can we go to chapel?'

'Goodness,' said her mother. 'It's awful,' she said to

Eiry. 'I never think, you know. We always went at Craig Wen, when I was married to Rheinallt.'

'There's no Welsh chapel in Oxford,' said Eiry.

'I suppose that's why I forget,' said Rhiannon. 'But there are plenty of other chapels, United Reform and so on. I ought to find out about services. I will, Heledd, I promise.'

As they neared home, having parted with Eiry at the college flats, Rhiannon said to Heledd, 'We'll be able to go to Horeb next Sunday, won't we, if the snow's cleared.'

'Might – might we not go, because of the snow?'

Rhiannon put her arm round her daughter's shoulders. 'We're going to do our very very best not to be put off. We know how much Craig Wen means to you. That reminds me, I must phone Mrs Williams Bryn Teg. She's sure to have room for us at this time of year.'

Heledd's heart thumped uneasily.

The week before half term seemed interminable. Heledd went to school, watched the weather and listened for the phone, in between dipping with fascinated dread into the book about Lawrence of Arabia and listening to the trains struggling up and down the line at the bottom of the garden.

Victoria and Isabel were in high spirits as they packed up vast quantities of clothes and cosmetics to take with them to London.

Rhiannon had booked rooms with Mrs Williams Bryn Teg, a double for herself and David and a single for Heledd, despite Heledd's protesting that it would save money if she slept at Craig Wen. Heledd took out her own suitcase and packed some jumpers and underwear on top of her father's letter and books. She also took out her portfolio of paintings and began to look through them, but had to stop in case – in case of what, she did not quite know. In case they were not true, perhaps. In case, all the time, she had been painting what she wanted to see rather than what was really there. According to the author of the book she was reading, that was what T. E. Lawrence had done when writing *Seven Pillars of Wisdom.* He had written the history of the Arab Revolt not as an accurate, dispassionate record but as an exciting adventure story with himself as the hero. But if that were true how could her father admire him so?

The ringing of the telephone cut ruthlessly through the cheerful row of *Top of the Pops* on television on Friday night. Isabel and Victoria had dragged Heledd in to watch because Catatonia were going to be on. Heledd knew with sinking heart that this was the call from Wales she had been dreading. She reached quickly for the phone to answer it but the call had already been taken on the study extension. A few moments later David put his head round the door and said, 'Isabel, Victoria, could you come through for a minute?'

His face was grave. Isabel and Victoria stood up at once and followed him. 'I'm terribly sorry,' Heledd heard him say, before the study door closed. As she switched off the television she heard Isabel give a great wailing cry, and then break down into sobs.

The study door swung open and Isabel rushed out shouting, 'I don't want you! I want my Mum!' She stumbled upstairs, sobbing, with Rhiannon following saying, 'I'm so sorry, my darling.'

Before Heledd could slip away to her room David came out of the study followed by an irate Victoria.

'She knew!' Victoria was saying furiously. 'The cow. The bitch. She knew. I thought we were doing a bit too well, seeing her last weekend as well as at half term. She's done this on purpose, she's strung us along because she didn't have the bottle to tell us to our face that she'd rather go off to New York with bleeding Christopher than spend a week with her own daughters.'

'Calm down, Vix,' said David wearily. 'I wish you wouldn't swear like that.' He tried to put his arms round his daughter but she shrugged him off. Upstairs, Isabel had slammed the bedroom door on Rhiannon and was screaming, 'Go away! I want my Mum! I want my own Mum!'

'I'm going to be stuck here on my own all week,' raged Victoria. 'Justin's going off with Rog and Rich in the camper tomorrow – oh! I could kill her!' She looked up. 'I'm going to phone Just. I'm not stopping here, I'll go up the wall. I'm going with them.'

'You and three boys? In this weather? No you are not,' said David. He caught Heledd's eye and sighed helplessly. Heledd knew the sigh meant, sorry, love, we won't be able to go to Craig Wen now.

We could all go, she thought. Mrs Williams might have an extra room. She knew at once that the idea was unworkable. Isabel and Victoria would never consent, and even if they did there wasn't room for them all in the car.

She listened to David trying to talk Victoria down from her temper, feeling embarrassed and for some reason ashamed. Presently she picked up her book and went quietly upstairs to her bedroom, which was not really her room, but Isabel's. She sat on the bed for a long while, listening to the trains.

16

'And to cap it all,' said Victoria, setting tiny cups of bitter, cardamom-flavoured Arabic coffee on the mosaic table before Richard and Ben at the Road to Damascus café early the following morning, 'when we all wake up this morning, after Iz has howled all night, blow me if the precious Princess hasn't disappeared! Empty bed, suitcase gone, note on the dressing table. She's taken the train home to Wales, and she probably won't be back, so Iz can have her room back. Nobody saw her leave. Rhiannon and David look as though they've been jemmied. I was so glad to get out of the house, you wouldn't believe. Thank God you're all still here.'

She drew a chair up to their table and sat down. From behind the counter the proprietor, a dark, round-faced young man known as Arty, called, 'If you're here to work, Vix, you're here to work, not sit and gossip. Nothing like hard work for getting through troubled times.'

'I said that's what'd happen, didn't I,' said Justin,

eating the foam off the top of his cappuccino with a spoon. 'I said you'd wake up one morning and find her gone, and only a few white feathers, and all that.'

'Gosh, Justin,' said Richard. 'How poetic! You have a soul after all!'

'And were there feathers?' asked Ben.

'No, of course not,' said Victoria with a giggle. 'Only she'd left some pictures out. Paintings of where she used to live. They were amazing.'

'What, amazingly good or amazingly bad?'

'Well, good, but they were kind of frightening. Big landscapes with mountains, and weird pools of water and great gashes of black rock.'

'Slate quarries,' said Justin, who knew Snowdonia from climbing holidays.

'And she'd done one of her dad, he looked just like her. She's been wanting to go home, all this time,' added Victoria suddenly. 'You can tell. She never thinks of anything else.'

'Poor Heledd,' said Ben quietly.

'They were going down there this week, her and Rhiannon and Dad,' said Victoria, going behind the counter and beginning to spoon fresh coffee into the espresso machine scoop. 'I suppose she realised that'd be off, when Mum phoned last night and said we couldn't come to London for half term after all. They'd never leave us in Oxford on our own.'

'So she went anyway,' said Richard. 'Good for her. It has always been clear to me that Heledd is a person with hidden depths.'

'But surely,' said Ben, 'they won't just leave her?'

'I think the idea is that Rhiannon will go down to Wales after her, and Dad will stay here with me and Iz,' said Victoria. 'And they've phoned a neighbour to meet her train, or something. But Iz is in such a state at the moment, she won't let Rhiannon out of her sight. I don't know why they don't all go to Wales, all three of them. I'd be perfectly all right at home on my own. I did say to Dad that I might join you lot in the camper, but he wouldn't wear it. What, you and three boys? Not likely,' he said.'

'Four boys,' corrected Roger, coming into the café at that moment. 'Ben's coming too. You and four boys sounds fine by me, Vix. Come on, cough up,' he said to the others. 'I've just put thirty quid's worth of diesel in the waggon, not to mention the oil.'

'I feel so sorry for David and Rhiannon,' said Richard. 'They never get the chance to be together without you girls.'

'Tough,' said Victoria, making cappuccinos for herself and Roger, and an espresso for Arty.

'Don't be mean,' said Richard. 'They are in love. It's one of the great Oxford love affairs, according to my mum.' He took a sip of coffee from the tiny gilt-rimmed cup, smiling dreamily over the rim at them all. 'I've had an idea,' he said. 'I have had such a good idea. Didn't I hear that Lawrence of Arabia was born not far from where Heledd lives?'

'We're going to Dorset, remember?' said Roger, rolling his eyes. 'It was all your idea in the first place.'

'We can't go to Wales, there's too much snow,' said Justin.

'It just seems rather ridiculous,' said Richard, 'to start

with the place where Lawrence's life ended rather than where it began.'

'I'm not coming with you to Wales,' said Victoria. 'It'll be freezing.'

'Oh yes you are,' said Richard. 'And so is Isabel.'

'Don't be crazy! Dad and Rhiannon would never let us!'

'I bet you they will,' said Richard, finishing his coffee and jumping to his feet.

'Well,' said David.

He was tempted, they could see.

'If it weren't for the weather,' he said.

'It's thawing,' said Richard. 'The roads are clear.'

'They may well be clear down here,' said David, 'but Snowdonia may be quite a different matter. The people on the farm next door to Craig Wen say the roads are fairly clear there at the moment but what if it snows again?'

Rhiannon was saying nothing. She sat in the biggest kitchen chair, rocking an exhausted Isabel on her knee. Isabel's head lay on Rhiannon's shoulder, her thin legs were hooked over the arm of the chair and she was sucking her thumb.

'Oh God,' said David. 'What do you think, Rhiannon?'

'We will be terribly, terribly responsible, Doctor Middleton, I promise,' said Richard. 'If the weather's too bad, we'll come straight home, and bring Heledd with us.'

'If she'll come,' said Victoria.

'Heledd's nearly sixteen,' said Rhiannon. 'She's lived

in Snowdonia all her life. She's much less at risk in the mountains that any of you people. But there'll be a lot of work to do at Craig Wen. You'd better take plenty of mops and brushes with you. And sleeping bags.' She smiled tiredly at David. 'I don't think they need stay there, though. The boys could stay at the Youth Hostel in Bethesda, and the girls can have our booking with Mrs Williams.'

'Oh good, I knew you'd agree,' said Richard.

'Well, all right,' said David. 'But no sex!'

'Wouldn't dream of it.'

'No dope!'

'Not even a cigarette.'

'No alcohol!'

'Certainly not, with a Moslem in our company.'

'The trouble with you, Richard Clare, is you're too bloody glib for your own good.' said David. 'Ben's parents may not be at all happy with the idea. I mean, isn't it Ramadan about now? You must all get your parents' permission too, before we take things any further.'

'My parents have gone on holiday,' said Justin. 'It won't make any difference to them.'

'Ma's finishing a book,' said Richard. 'It won't make any difference to her where we go, Dorset or Tremadog or Tashkent, which is where Dad is at the moment.'

'Ben?'

'My parents won't mind,' said Ben hesitantly. 'Ramadan is over. The only other thing –'

'We'll need you, too, Isabel,' said Richard, 'to chaperone Victoria, you know.'

Victoria groaned. Isabel took her thumb out of her mouth and said, 'Will she still have the pony?'

'What?'

'She used to have a pony,' said Isabel. 'She told me. And a goat.'

'I believe the pony's still alive,' said Rhiannon. 'Though she must be getting on for thirty by now. She lives at the Davieses down the mountain from Craig Wen. Heledd would take you to see her, I'm sure.'

'That's settled, then,' said Richard.

'Rhiannon, are we off our heads?' asked David. 'Look at the weather!'

'Probably,' said Rhiannon. She ran her fingers through her tousled hair. 'I wish she hadn't done this,' she said. 'But somehow I'm not surprised. I've even been expecting it, you know?'

'It was our fault,' said Victoria. 'Going on about not having enough room. So it ought to be us that goes to see if she's all right.'

Rhiannon said, 'I don't think it's a matter of being anybody's fault. She's just terribly unhappy still.' She pressed her hand over her mouth as though trying not to weep.

'Darling,' said David. 'Darling, please don't. Look, we'll go too. The kids can go in the van and we'll follow on in the car.'

Rhiannon shook her head. 'It's not me Heledd wants,' she said. 'It never has been.' She breathed in deeply and blew her nose. 'Sorry.' She stood up and let David put his arms round her. 'It's best that the children go after her,' she said. 'But I want to ask them to wait until tomorrow before setting off. Can you bear that, Roger? It's too late to go today, it'll be dark before you get to Shrewsbury. And I must write Heledd a letter which I'd like you to give to her. There's something I need to tell her.'

PART II

WALES – *CYMRU*

17

'Wake up, me duck, we'll be in Crewe in five minutes.'

Heledd came to with a start. The lady guard who had sold her a can of apple juice from a trolley somewhere between Wolverhampton and Stafford was grinning down at her. 'I wish I could sleep like that on the train. It rattles around worse than a camel. You being met?'

Heledd shook her head. She made herself whisper, 'I'm going to Bangor.'

'They'll hold the connection, we're only twenty minutes late. Better'n when it's fine sometimes!' The lady guard peered out of the train window into the murky daylight. 'Gordon Bennet, what a day!' She wandered away down the carriage, exchanging cheerful remarks with the other passengers. It was as though the dreary weather had made them all feel quite sociable.

Crewe, then Chester, then Wales, thought Heledd. She sat up in her seat and rubbed her eyes. At long last. The journey seemed endless. This particular train might only be twenty minutes late but it was a later connection from Birmingham than she had hoped for, because the train from Oxford had been delayed by a points failure. It had sat in the station for what seemed hours. Heledd had huddled as unobtrusively as possible in her seat, expecting every moment to see her mother and David running onto the platform looking for her.

What would they do when they found her note? Call the police? No, Heledd had realised as the train eventually pulled out of the station and chugged slowly along the line past the end of the Middletons' garden. What they would probably do was phone Mrs Davies Tanygraig and ask her to meet the train at Bangor. They'd probably arrange for her to stay at Tanygraig as well. She would have to be on her guard against that. But she had to face facts. There was no point in hoping to live at Craig Wen all solitary and undiscovered like Robinson Crusoe. Too many people knew her. But she did not intend to let anyone stop her staying there. From the moment that telephone call had come for Isabel and Victoria last night she had known what she must do, and now there was no turning back.

Going home. The very words poured relief and joy into her veins. It was as though her head was clear for the first time since her father died. All the irrelevance of her Oxford life was behind her for ever. It didn't matter that she would not be sixteen until July, or eighteen for another two years or that she had only about fifty pounds left in the whole world. She would manage somehow. She'd walk into Bethesda every day and scrub floors if necessary. She'd build up a new herd of goats and sell the milk cheap to all the asthmatic children in the quarry villages. She'd grow vegetables and keep hens just as she had done when her father was alive. She'd make Welsh cakes and sell them in Bangor market. And every day she would wake up and there would be Moel Wynion and Y Drosgl and the Carneddau, and the Menai Straits and Anglesey and the sea. And there her father would be too, quite nearby under his neat brown mound of earth in the little graveyard of Horeb chapel. She would be able to go and talk to him every day.

It was well after two o'clock when the Chester train,

full of shoppers and people laden with climbing gear, crossed the border. Presently the stations had bilingual place name signs and there were people in the carriage talking to each other in Welsh. Heledd found herself almost tearful as she heard her beloved language being spoken all around her once more. The passengers were discussing quite ordinary things, like the bargain they had got from Curry's, or their chances of getting home before the snow started again, but to Heledd it all sounded like the most glorious poetry.

Heledd pressed her nose against the window looking for familiar landmarks, but it was impossible to see much through the grimy glass. There was snow on the fields and a low mist on the sea. A main road ran between the railway line and the sea, and the cars that raced along it seemed to be going much faster than the train.

Prestatyn, Rhyl, Abergele, then the last half hour. Train journeys were strange; it was as though your life stopped as you counted the passing stations. It was impossible to think about any of the things you knew you ought to be thinking about. She wiped the condensation from the window again and again, peering out at the snow-streaked hills, but they seemed far away and unreal in the murky light. It was as though she was dreaming them. Her elation began to ebb, to be replaced by a sense of dread. But suddenly they had passed Llandegai and were in the tunnel and a voice was announcing bilingually that this was Bangor and that they apologised for the late arrival of the train.

She was almost afraid to alight from the train. The station was lit up, throwing its surroundings into darkness, but the platform seemed deserted. It took a cough from an impatient hiker to make her jump down. She glanced about nervously but there was no sign of any of the Davieses Tanygraig, or anyone else she knew.

She followed the other disembarking passengers over the bridge and out into the station forecourt. She could see no familiar vehicles parked in the car park. Her breath misted on the chilly air and she put down her suitcase to fasten her duffel coat, her cold fingers fumbling nervously. She had been so certain that her mother would phone the Davieses and ask them to meet her off the train that she had not planned what to do if they did not.

They must be out, she thought. Perhaps lambing has started early this year. Perhaps they're snowed in after all. If they are, Craig Wen must be snowed in too.

Slowly, her brain began to work again. It would be cowardly to panic now, when she was so nearly home. It wasn't as though there would be any problem getting herself home from Bangor, she used to do it every day after school. She looked at her watch. It was twenty to four. If she walked down to the town clock she could catch the four-thirty bus which made the round trip to Bethesda via a number of outlying villages including the one nearest to Craig Wen. If the bus was running, the snow couldn't be too bad. After that it was only a mile up the track to the cottage.

There was plenty of time, so she could go to the supermarket and buy some groceries. She gave thanks that she had thought to withdraw more money from the bank on the way to Oxford station that morning. The railway ticket had cost far more than she had anticipated. The man in the ticket office had given her a strange look when she had asked for a single to Bangor, because it cost nearly as much as a return. He'd remember, for sure, if anyone asked, but evidently nobody had.

It was a relief, really. It indicated that people weren't worrying about her. They accepted that she was doing the right thing, and that she was quite capable of organising things like buses and shopping. She began to make a mental list. Matches and candles would be a good idea, firelighters too, and soap and milk and bread. Then the bus, and the walk home. Tomorrow she would set Craig Wen to rights, and on Monday she would walk into Bethesda and start looking for a job.

It was only as she was loading her supermarket shopping into carrier bags that she remembered that she had given the key to Craig Wen to Tristan.

'*Oes gen ti broblem?*' The supermarket checkout girl, looking at her stricken face with friendly concern, was asking her if there was a problem. '*Wedi anghofio rhywbeth?*' Had she forgotten something?

Despite the people on the train it still surprised her to be addressed in her mother tongue after all those weeks in Oxford. She shook her head, dropping some change in her confusion.

Was she stupid? she wondered as she scrabbled clumsily on the floor after the rolling coins. How could she have forgotten? For the past two weeks she had been worrying non-stop about giving the key to Tristan, but then at the crucial moment, when she really needed to remember, she had forgotten all about him. She hadn't even checked that she still had the key.

But if I had remembered, I might not have come, she thought, straightening up and muttering an apology to the check-out girl and the next customer in the queue. Anyway, he won't be there. How would he get himself from Oxford to a strange cottage in the middle of nowhere? He's probably lost the key already. It doesn't matter. I'll get in somehow. Dad was always locking himself out and he always managed. And if all else fails the Davieses have a spare key.

The bus was full of people going home after their Saturday afternoon shopping. Heledd found a seat next to a hippyish-looking woman with a baby on her knee and hid herself behind her carrier bags. A group of girls from her old school waved at her and nudged each other but did not sit near enough to chat. She could hear mutterings of *'Merch Rheinallt'* from other passengers but she kept her eyes on the sleeping baby to avoid their curious looks.

The bus driver knew where to stop for her to get off, at the bottom of the track to Craig Wen. He said 'Ta ta, *cyw*,' as she thanked him and jumped down into the snowy hedge bottom. She waited as the bus drove away, breathing in deeply, feeling the cold air sharp on her face. The mist had cleared and the sky was striped with pink and gold and dark blue as the sun set. The landscape glowed rosily in the evening light, patches of snow flashing on the black scree slopes. The lights of Anglesey flickered in the distance across the Strait. It was very quiet. Not an owl hooted, not a fox barked.

The track to Craig Wen wound slowly uphill, bordered by a skinny hedge on one side and a slate fence on the other. Snow had drifted up against the hedge but had been impacted underfoot by the wheels of a farm vehicle. The tyre marks were still crisp, as though recent. Mr Davies must have driven up the hillside looking out for his sheep, she thought. It was impossible to tell if anyone else had walked up the track recently. Picking up her suitcase in one hand and her supermarket carrier bags in the other, Heledd set off.

It always seemed a long walk home to Craig Wen when you were carrying shopping, but once you reached the top of the first rise you could look across a shallow valley and see the cottage tucked under an outcrop of rock on the far hillside. It was much easier after that. Heledd's heart began to beat fast. She felt warm and energetic despite the cold. The words of another of Ann Griffiths's hymns came to her: *Ffordd a'i henw yn rhyfeddol,* 'A way whose name is wonderful', which always made her think of the lane to Craig Wen in the summer when the foxgloves were out. Her father could sing the tune better than she could. She could hear him now.

She set down her bags and rubbed her fist across her face. She mustn't weep. She must go on. She was nearly home now.

She picked up her bags again and began to hurry, stumbling on the stones hidden beneath the snow. This was the steepest bit, but any moment in the distance she would be able to see Craig Wen quietly waiting for her.

And there it was, the last of the light catching on its whitewashed stone walls. Heledd paused to make the most of her first sight of home after so many months, then gasped aloud.

Tristan must have found the cottage after all. Or

someone must have done, because there was a light in the window, and smoke curling out of the chimney, and a Land Rover parked outside the door.

18

Don't let it be Tristan, she prayed as she struggled tiredly along the last few hundred yards of track to the cottage. Let it be Mr Davies Tanygraig lighting a fire to give the place an airing.

But as she approached the cottage she realised that the Land Rover couldn't be Mr Davies Tanygraig's, it was far too new. She paused, her heart beating very fast. What if someone else – not Tristan – had broken in and was living there – somebody dangerous? Old stories of isolated houses taken over by drug dealers surfaced ominously in her memory.

She gripped her bags and tiptoed quietly across the patch of snow in front of the cottage, making for the stable, but at that moment the front door opened and a bulky young man in a sheepskin coat came out. He stopped dead when he saw Heledd. An expression of utter consternation came over his face. For several moments he stared at her speechlessly, then his face relaxed and he gave a shaky laugh.

'Hell fire!' said the young man in Welsh. 'You gave me a turn! Just for a moment I thought – *Iesu Grist!* It's Heledd, isn't it? Sorry! I'm a fool! My God, you're like your Dad!'

He came towards her, hand outstretched. 'Griff Jenkins, Arts Council of Wales. I wrote to your Aunt Sioned.'

The one who wanted to turn Craig Wen into a poets' retreat. Heledd shook hands guardedly.

'I was passing,' said Griff Jenkins. 'I couldn't resist coming to have a look at Craig Wen. I admire your father beyond all. I didn't know you'd let the place.'

Looking past him Heledd saw Tristan standing in the doorway, his jaw moving as he chewed a wad of gum. 'He was calling me a squatter just now,' he remarked.

'Rheinallt's sister didn't say anything about a tenant,' said Griff Jenkins defensively.

'What's it to you?' Tristan was speaking English, Heledd noticed, although Griff was speaking Welsh.

'All right, all right, I'm sorry,' said Griff Jenkins.

Heledd thought, I can't stay here. I shouldn't have come. You don't just turn up at a house with a tenant and expect to be allowed in. I'll have to go to Tanygraig.

But Tristan was already standing back and saying, 'Are you coming in, then? It's freezing out here.' At least she qualified for being addressed in Welsh. Griff Jenkins followed Heledd over the threshold.

'Cuppa tea?' asked Tristan.

She nodded gratefully. He gave her a sardonic grin. He was still as unshaven and filthy as he had been when Heledd had last seen him on St. Mary's Tower, but the feverish glitter had gone from his eyes.

'I'll fill the kettle,' said Griff. 'Is there a tap in the back kitchen?'

'If there is, I haven't found it,' said Tristan. 'I bin getting water from the stream.'

'Right you are,' said Griff, ignoring Tristan's

unfriendly tone. 'Hope I'm not barging in,' he said to Heledd. 'There's just something I want to ask, then I'll be off and leave you two in peace. Down for half term, are you, Heledd?' Something about the way he winked and grinned dismayed Heledd. Surely people wouldn't think she had run away to be with Tristan?

Aunt Sioned would.

Tristan was stacking more logs on the fire, his face flushed from the heat, so she could not see how he was taking this.

She said, 'We use water from the rainwater butt for washing. We heat it up in the range.'

Tristan took the gum out of his mouth and threw it into the fire. 'That a hint?'

'No,' she said tiredly, putting her bags down.

'You hardly see these old ranges in full working order any more,' said Griff. 'Not for heating water, anyway. Doesn't it leak?'

'Not very much. Dad welded it.'

Her father had been very proud of the iron cooking range, which he had restored with the advice of a man from the Welsh Folk Museum. It had an oven on one side of the fire, a water boiler with a tap on the other, and a hook on a chain for hanging pots and pans over the flames. A bread oven with an iron door was built into the side of the chimney. The range had always been Heledd's responsibility. It was her job to riddle all the soot out of the flues and clear the ashes out of the grate. She had become an expert at regulating the heat of the oven by adjusting the dampers, and she knew exactly how long to fire the bread oven before scraping out the cinders and putting the bread to bake. It was part of her old life, and she felt a terrible confusion that having come all this way she could not be on her own to remember it all and to start living it again in peace.

What did you expect? she asked herself. You gave Tristan the key. How could you have forgotten?

'Sit down, *bach,* you look shattered,' said Griff. 'It's a long old train journey from Oxford, isn't it? If I can find a bucket I'll fill the boiler.' He went outside, carrying a torch with him.

'I haven't touched anything,' said Tristan, addressing Heledd rather truculently. 'I mean I've swept up a bit and aired the blankets and that but I haven't been in any boxes of books or papers or anything and I wouldn't let him either.'

It was true that the kitchen seemed tidy and warm, if rather smelly from Tristan's clothes and a ragged supermarket carrier full of empty tuna and baked bean tins.

'My Nain was always on about airing blankets,' said Tristan. 'You remember that kind of thing, don't you?'

Heledd lifted her father's wooden armchair nearer to the fire and sat down. Griff came in with a bucketful of rainwater and she showed him how to lift the lid of the boiler and pour the water in, listening to the familiar sizzle as it hit the hot metal.

'Mind you, what you need is total immersion,' said Griff to Tristan. 'I'll run you down to the sports centre in Bethesda if you like. You can have a shower and put your clothes through the launderette at the same time.'

'Mind your own effing business.'

'All right, all right, only trying to be helpful. Funny kind of lodger you've got, Heledd, if you don't mind my saying so. Does your Aunt Sioned know about him? She didn't say anything to me.'

'It's my house,' said Heledd coldly. 'I can invite who I like.'

'Of course you can,' said Griff, backing down. 'Sorry if I was rude. Sorry,' he said again, addressing Tristan. Why doesn't he go? Heledd wondered. He can see he's not wanted. What's he after?

She tried to remember what her mother had said about the scheme he had put to Aunt Sioned, but the heat of the fire was making her eyelids droop. Now that she was sitting down she knew her energy had come to an end. There were all sorts of questions she ought to be asking, but she could not sort them out in her head. All she could manage was to sit there and let Tristan bring her a mug of tea and digestive biscuits in a torn packet. Oh, she was tired. If she could just rest for a while . . . but she mustn't fall asleep, she must find out what this Griff wanted. Because he was looking for something, it was obvious from the way his eyes darted about the room as he chatted about kitchen ranges.

Heledd forced herself awake, and made herself finish her tea. Tristan was standing at the table filling a paraffin lamp, watched by Griff. Had he trimmed the wick? Before she could ask she heard Tristan bang the can of paraffin down and say aggressively, 'I don't know nothing. I'm only staying here. Does that have to make me a fully paid up member of the Rheinallt fan club? And even if I was, do you think I'd go poking around in his things?'

'Rheinallt may not be important to you,' said Griff, 'but he's very important to practically everybody else in Wales.' He turned to Heledd. 'Your aunt tells me that before he died your father was working on a new poem. A long poem, she said. You don't know anything about it, do you?'

The manuscript of the poem was in Heledd's suitcase which Griff had propped on the ladder leading to the loft.

'He put all his last strength into it, she said. There he'd be in bed scribbling away something frantic.'

Trust Aunt Sioned, thought Heledd.

'You must trim the wick before lighting the lamp,' she said to Tristan. 'Otherwise it'll smoke.'

'Believe it or not,' said Tristan, 'I knew that. I got a penknife somewhere.'

'So you don't know anything about the poem? It's got to be somewhere,' persisted Griff. 'Surely he wouldn't have destroyed it? It must be somewhere.'

Tristan shrugged. Griff came over to the hearth and sat opposite Heledd on the old chapel pew her father had placed there instead of a settle. 'It must have been packed away in his papers,' he said. 'But you must know about it, Heledd. And you must know how important it is to us all. To Wales. Our great poet's last work.' He paused, and coughed diffidently. 'Look, the thing is, I'm writing about him, see? I think it was shameful, all the things they did to try to discredit him. I want to expose it all. There might be a television programme too.'

'My father would not have wanted that,' said Heledd.

'But surely you want him cleared? You know they deliberately tried to destroy his reputation so that people wouldn't make a hero of him.'

'He was cleared,' said Heledd. After a moment she added, 'He was a poet. He didn't want to be a hero. And he said you should forgive people.'

'If he didn't want to be a hero he shouldn't have

stayed up that bloody mast for three days without food or water until the police backed down,' said Griff, jumping angrily to his feet and making the chapel pew rock. 'He nearly died of hypothermia and they never forgave him. They were out to get him from that moment on. He was – he *is* a hero, he can't back out of that.'

'He was a bloody fool,' said Tristan. 'But he was her father. So you leave her alone.'

'He was more than her father,' said Griff. 'He gave himself to Wales. I can't believe she doesn't know about that poem.'

I mustn't let him frighten me, thought Heledd, holding on to the arms of her chair. If she admitted to having the poem what might happen to her? Might Griff open her suitcase and seize the manuscript? He was a big person, he could overpower her easily. Yet she could not lie about it. Her father would not have wanted her to lie. And although Griff was big he did not look cruel.

'I know about the poem,' she said. 'It's called "Feet of Sand".'

'You do!' said Griff. 'I knew it! Good on you, Heledd! Have you got it? Can we see it? What did you say it was called?'

'*Traed Tywod*. Feet of Sand.'

'Feet of what? Come on, Heledd, you must let us see it.'

'No,' said Heledd. 'He said it was for me. He sent it to me in his last letter.'

'But he can't have meant you not to publish it!'

'I might publish it one day,' said Heledd, standing up. She went over to the loft ladder and grasped the handle of her suitcase to keep it safe.

'Heledd!'

'Leave her alone,' said Tristan, moving round the table so that he was standing between Heledd and Griff. 'That's what you came for, isn't it? All that rubbish about a poets' retreat was just an excuse. Quite a little coup it would be, wouldn't it, discovering an unpublished poem by Rheinallt. Get you on telly in a minute.'

'That's not true!'

'You'd better push off,' said Tristan. 'She's had enough, and so have I.' He turned to Heledd. 'If you want me to push off I will, but it'd help if I could I stay on a couple of nights. It'd be easier to get a lift on a Monday.'

'No,' said Heledd. 'That's not why I came. You can stay as long as you like. Eiry told me about your Nain –'

'You can't stay here with him,' said Griff. 'Your mother wouldn't like it. Or on the other hand, knowing her and her fancy men, she probably wouldn't mind.'

Heledd felt as though her face had been slapped. This was the kind of thing she had heard her Aunt Sioned say about her mother, behind her back.

'Sorry,' said Griff. 'Look, I'm sorry. I didn't mean it. I'm upset, I am. I really wanted to see the poem. Rheinallt means everything to me!'

'And your career,' said Tristan.

'That's not true! Don't you speak to me in that tone of voice!'

'It isn't what you think,' said Heledd, her voice shaking. 'The poem. It isn't about Wales. It's about Lawrence of Arabia. And it's dedicated to my mother.'

'But you said he gave it to you,' said Griff, turning on her aggressively like a television interviewer trying to trap an evasive politician.

Heledd was silent.

'If he dedicated it to Rhiannon, why did he give it to you and not her?'

I don't know, thought Heledd. Still clutching the suitcase she stumbled to her chair and sat down again. It was a mistake, she thought. But perhaps it wasn't a mistake.

'It's none of your business,' she heard Tristan telling Griff. 'Going on at her like some bloody tabloid journalist. Why should she owe you an explanation?'

Griff carried on as though Tristan had not spoken. 'I can't believe he gave it to you. You'd just burned all his clothes on a bonfire. How did he know you wouldn't do the same with the poem? Didn't know that, did you,' he said to Tristan. 'We've got a little arsonist on our hands here. I knew there was something funny about that business at Bryan Middleton's house.'

'For Christ's sake,' said Tristan. 'Why don't you pick on somebody your own weight? And check your sources,' he added, as Heledd sat helplessly shaking her head. 'If anything she's ever done is any business of yours, which it isn't.'

'Everything that happened to Rheinallt in his last months alive is important.' But the conviction was draining from Griff's voice. 'Sorry,' he muttered. 'You're right. I shouldn't have – But Rheinallt's sister said –' he mouthed the words over Heledd's head – 'she's a bit mad, you know – didn't speak for months when her father was in and out of prison and hospital. She just didn't speak. Not even to him.'

Tristan made no response, giving him no encouragement to continue with these confidences.

'Just so you know what you're getting yourself into,' Griff said in more audible tones.

Heledd tried to rouse herself. What were they saying? Had they asked her something? But shock and fatigue had numbed her brain. She let the suitcase slide off her knee to the floor and closed her eyes, blocking out the presence of the two men. She must have slept for a little while, because the next thing she noticed was that the shouting had stopped. Tristan was kneeling at her feet, trying to turn the tap of the range boiler to run off some hot water into the enamel washing up bowl.

'Well, I am doing my best,' he said, seeing her open her eyes. The tap gave suddenly and a dollop of scalding brownish water spurted into the bowl, splashing Tristan so that he yelped. Heledd watched him carry the bowl to the table and dunk the dirty mugs into it. She looked around the shadowy kitchen, so dear, so familiar. She was home at last. But it wasn't the same. Griff had spoiled it.

'He's gone,' said Tristan, seeing her look round anxiously. 'That Griff. Vulture. Can't wait to start picking at the corpse. I mean – shit! Sorry!'

'*Dim ots*,' said Heledd. 'It doesn't matter.' It was true, after all. She felt grateful to Tristan for helping her to stand up to Griff. He seemed much more sensible than he had done in Oxford; it must be because he was no longer starving. What a good thing I sent him that money, she thought. And I'm not sorry I gave him the key now, either.

'You are staying, are you?' said Tristan, putting the clean mugs to drain on the table. 'If I'd known you were coming I'd have aired your bed. You can bunk in with me, if you like, seeing as it's what they all expect –' Seeing Heledd's face, he broke off. 'Sorry – joke – sorry, forget I spoke.'

I suppose I should go to Tanygraig, thought Heledd wearily. The prospect of having to explain herself to the Davieses was dreadful. The very thought made her want to fall asleep again right where she was. The fire was warm, and a there was a good pile of dry logs in the basket – she remembered that there had been plenty left over from last winter, stacked up in the barn outside.

I'm fine here for tonight, she thought. I'll unpack a blanket. I'll go to Tanygraig tomorrow. As she was trying to decide whether or not she needed to go to the *tŷ bach* she drifted off to sleep again.

She was woken by the sound of a vehicle drawing up outside the cottage. Opening her eyes she saw Tristan sitting at the kitchen table with her suitcase open in front of him. He held the manuscript of her father's poem in his hand and was reading it with brooding concentration by the light of the paraffin lamp.

Then someone knocked loudly on the kitchen door and Tristan jumped. He saw Heledd watching him and dropped his eyes. 'Yeah, well, sorry.'

'Who's in there?' called the voice of Mr Davies Tanygraig from outside. 'Is that you, Heledd?'

'Oh God,' said Tristan. He tossed the sheets of manuscript back into the suitcase and rubbed his hands over his face, which seemed to be wet. 'Oh God,' he said again. He sniffed deeply, and wiped his nose on his sleeve. Then he swayed forwards across the table until his head was resting on his forearms.

Heledd pulled herself slowly to her feet as the door opened.

19

An hour later, in Oxford, Rhiannon put the telephone down and turned to her husband. 'She's at Tanygraig,' she said wearily. 'Mr Davies brought her back with him.'

'She won't be very happy about that,' said David. 'Still, I suppose it's for the best, until she's got Craig Wen warmed up again.'

'That's not the problem,' said Rhiannon. 'It's the boy. The boy who is squatting at Craig Wen. A hippy, Mrs Davies says. She says Heledd says he's homeless and she gave him the key. And David, listen, Mrs Davies says he's Welsh and his name is –'

'Oh God,' said David. 'Don't tell me.'

'Of all the things that might possibly happen,' said Rhiannon, 'the last thing I ever thought of was that Heledd would run off with a boy.'

'Who, or what,' said David the following morning, looking at the name painted along the cream sides of the camper van, 'is Wodheiha, and how do you pronounce it?'

'You'll never guess,' said Roger, leaning out of the driver's seat window. 'Lawrence of Arabia's camel. Nothing to do with me.'

'She was a noble beast!' cried Richard from the back of the van where he was pushing Victoria's bag under the bench seat. 'She had won many races, and pulled him out of many a quicksand. It's all there, in *Seven Pillars*, so she deserves to have our chariot named after her. She was cream, too.'

'The only woman he ever loved, by the sound of it,' said Roger.

'Well, I hope you're not going to race this Wodheiha,' said David. 'Keep to a nice steady jog-trot, please. No exceeding the speed limit, and plenty of oasis stops.' He turned as Victoria and Isabel came out of the house followed by Rhiannon. 'And for Pete's sake, watch the weather. Vix, have you got your mobile phone?'

'You bet,' said Victoria, slapping her hip.

'Good, but please don't start phoning your friends all over Europe. You know calls cost an arm and a leg. Let us know when you get there, that's the main thing. Now then, do you know the way?'

'Honestly, Dad,' said Victoria. 'You've asked that about fourteen times, and Rhiannon's made us at least fourteen maps. Hey!' She moved her elbow out of Richard's reach as he tried to help her into the back of the van. 'Who's sitting in the front, then?'

'We'll take turns, of course,' said Richard. 'I thought Isabel might like to come up front with me and Rog to start with, and we can swop round later.'

'Okay, as long as you don't hog it,' said Victoria, climbing into the van and sitting down next to Justin without acknowledging his presence. 'Gosh, I can hardly move for stuff. Look at all this food! Are we going to the Antarctic or what?'

'An army marches on its stomach,' said Richard. 'Napoleon. Don't laugh, Ben.'

'Richard, we are not an army.'

'Yes we are, we're a flying column off to relieve the garrison at Craig Wen. Like Lawrence liberating Aqaba.'

Richard was laughing and making faces at Ben as he spoke but his blue eyes were blazing.

'The Camel Corps, no doubt,' said David. 'But no blowing up railway lines, I beg.'

'If necessary, we will!'

Ben groaned. He began moving bags and cartons and climbing boots to make room for Victoria's feet. Searching amongst the luggage, he pulled out a bundle of red and white checked cloth and threw it at Richard, who immediately went scarlet.

'Not now, you idiot,' he said.

'You should have the courage of your convictions, English,' said Ben.

'All right,' said Richard, looking at Rhiannon who was talking to Roger by the open driver's seat door. He glared at Ben, then draped the cloth round his head and secured it with the head-rope. 'Satisfied? So what about you and your flaming convictions?'

In reply Ben held up what looked like a small, rolled-up carpet. 'It's my prayer mat,' he explained to a puzzled Isabel. 'You'll see.'

Rhiannon was saying to Roger, 'Please don't forget.' She handed him a letter in a long envelope and they heard him reply, 'No, I won't forget, Doctor Jones, I promise. Just a letter for Heledd,' he added to the others in response to their curious looks.

Presently they were driving away along the Woodstock Road, heading for the ring road and the A44 to Wales.

'Free at last,' said Victoria. 'Put your foot down, Roger.'

'We've got plenty of time, Vix. Sit back and enjoy the trip. Put some music on, Rich, will you?'

'Choose a tape, Isabel. Something appropriate for our Crusade,' said Richard. 'Oh no, wait, I tell you what.' He pushed a cassette into the player, flicking back the corner of his head cloth and giving Ben a defiant look. The van filled with the theme tune from the film *Lawrence of Arabia*. They all shouted in protest.

'Honest to God,' said Victoria. 'Is he living on our planet? Or in our century? Talk about day-dreaming. He's as bad as the Princess.'

Ben said, '*But the dreamers of the day are dangerous men.*'

'You reckon? Who said that, then?'

'Richard knows,' said Ben.

'Don't cry, my darling,' said David, taking Rhiannon into his arms as the camper van disappeared round the corner. He steered her indoors and closed the door. She leaned against him and wept into his shoulder for a few moments, then pressed her hands over her cheeks to compose herself.

'I'm sorry,' she said. 'It's all been a bit much. I do hope they'll be all right.'

'Of course they'll be all right. We need to let them grow up and deal with things on their own. I know Richard's got a mad look in his eye, but he's only acting. Roger and Ben will keep him in check you can be sure.'

'Should we have told them Tristan is there?'

'Tristan and Heledd!' said David. 'I can't believe it! Where can they have been meeting? And when? She must have been cutting school. But to run off with him!'

'This is all my fault,' said Rhiannon. 'I thought she'd

settle in Oxford. I thought she'd like it because Rheinallt liked it. I didn't understand how it's traumatised her to be uprooted.' She sighed. 'Oh God, I can't think straight. I wish I could see her. But I'm the last person she'll want to see. Oh God, and Sioned is going to create the most awful row when she finds out, the self-righteous old – oh God –'

'Darling, please don't cry,' said David. 'Come and sit down, I'll make some coffee. Then you can call Heledd at the Davieses. She ought to be up by now.'

Rhiannon sat down slowly, shaking her head. 'She won't want to talk to me. She wouldn't, last night. Mrs Davies said she was worried about Tristan. She was begging Mr Davies not to turn him out of Craig Wen.'

'Poor kid,' said David. 'She's all over the place, isn't she? Could it be that she's having a bit of a breakdown, do you think? I mean, there was that funny business at Bryan's – she would have walked right into that fire if Barbara and that other lad hadn't stopped her. What was that all about? Her father wasn't even dead.'

Rhiannon shook her head. Her mouth began to tremble again. 'I thought I understood, but I don't know any more. There doesn't seem to be anything I can do to help.'

'She'll be pleased to get a letter from you, though.'

'I've got a dreadful feeling,' said Rhiannon, 'I've made a terrible mistake writing that letter.'

'Darling – of course you haven't – please don't cry!'

'She's never loved me,' said Rhiannon. 'And now she never will.'

20

'There's no peace, Dad,' said Heledd, standing by her father's grave as the snow fell gently out of the low February sky. Inside the chapel, people were singing a hymn, *Sanctaidd*, with its familiar tune. Heledd had managed to escape from Tanygraig to attend the Sunday afternoon service, but had lost her nerve as she approached the chapel door. She had hidden in the telephone kiosk until the minister and all the congregation were safely inside. She was known to all of them, and their questions would have been unbearable.

The grave was a low earth mound, crusted with frozen snow, situated in the most exposed part of the graveyard looking out over the mountains. The new snow was settling like a clean, soft blanket over the dirty old stuff. Like a cloak, thought Heledd. A mourning cloak. She remembered the ones made from straw and shells in the Pitt-Rivers. Were mourning cloaks for the people who had died, or the people who mourned them? She had not thought to ask.

If I were to shed tears, thought Heledd, they would make little holes in the snow, they would sink down through the snow and the frozen earth, right down to where he's lying, and he might feel them for just one little moment.

But when it might be a relief to shed tears, she never could.

He's not down there anyway, said a brutal voice in her heart. He never was. There's only a pile of earth and a coffin and a few bones.

Her mother and her Aunt Sioned had quarrelled over

whether Heledd should be allowed to see her father in his coffin. Aunt Sioned thought it was morbid. Her mother had suggested that it might be important for Heledd to say goodbye to her father. She had left the scene of the argument, and when eventually she came down from her room the hearse had arrived and the coffin was being lifted aboard for the long slow drive north to Craig Wen and Capel Horeb.

Heledd and her mother and aunt had travelled in a second black car behind the hearse, discussing neutral topics like the weather with the driver. The journey had taken hours. Aunt Sioned had handed round barley sugar sweets to keep their strength up. Occasionally she would nod gravely out of the car window at the little clusters of people who seemed to be waiting at the roadside to watch the hearse pass by. It was like a state funeral, the papers said afterwards. Everyone wanted to pay their respects to a national hero.

Shivering, Heledd shook the fresh snow from her shoulders as though she could shake off the memory of the funeral. The wreaths and floral tributes lining the path to the grave, the packed chapel, the lane blocked with cars. Reporters and television cameramen with camcorders sitting like black crows on their shoulders. Nudgings and whisperings from the other mourners as Heledd and her mother took their seats in the front pew, hastily stilled as the Vice-Chancellor of the University leaned over to shake Rhiannon's hand and murmur condolences. Poets and politicians and academics climbing the steps to the Big Seat to pay tribute to their lost brother.

It all seemed to have nothing to do with her, or her

father. As the bier was wheeled out of the chapel at the end of the service the little bunch of white freesias she had placed on the coffin that morning had fallen to the ground. The only person to notice was her mother, who had, quite calmly, stood up and laid her hand on the minister's arm to stop him treading on it. Heledd scrambled down to pick it up, but could not bring herself to put it back with the other flowers. By the graveside, her Aunt Sioned had whispered to her to throw the freesias down on to the coffin, but Heledd could see nothing but television cameras and so had stood frozen, clutching the sweetly scented flowers in her gloveless hands. Later, she had slipped away from the Minister's house where the funeral tea was being held, round the chapel to the grave which had been covered with a tarpaulin. She had bent quickly and pushed the flowers under the canvas, but by then it seemed a pointless gesture.

It all seemed such a long time ago, but it was barely three months. November, her father had died. She might as well have died with him, for all the sense she could make of her life since. '*Stafell Gynddylan ys tywyll heno . . . . marw fy glyw; byw mi hunan . . . My Lord is dead, myself alive . . .*'

But it's not dark tonight, she thought. Tristan's there and he's lit a fire. And a candle. He's there on his own in the quiet just like I wanted to be. But he doesn't want me there and I've got nowhere else to go.

The hymn-singing in the chapel had stopped. Heledd heard the sound of doors being opened and people exclaiming at the sight of the falling snow. She hid round the corner, waiting for them all to leave so that she could go quietly back to the Davieses' farm. When the last car had driven cautiously away she came out of hiding and took refuge in the telephone kiosk once more. I'll phone Mam tonight, she thought drearily. I might as well go back to Oxford tomorrow. There's no point my staying here.

A feeling of desolation swept over her. She didn't want to go back to Oxford. She wanted to stay at Craig Wen, but by giving the key to Tristan she had made that impossible. I wish I'd died in that fire after all, she thought, then I'd be in heaven with Dad.

Except that God might not let her in after what she had done.

She began to push open the heavy door of the old-fashioned kiosk, then stepped back as another vehicle, some kind of van, came lumbering up the lane through the snow, its headlights on and its engine roaring in low gear. It shuddered to a halt a few yards from the kiosk and someone jumped out of the passenger seat.

'At least it'll tell us where we are,' said a voice that sounded weary from arguing. The door to the telephone kiosk was pulled wide open, and Heledd found herself staring at Richard Clare in his Arab head cloth.

At the sight of her he gave a loud yelp of delight and swept her off her feet in a huge hug. Whirling her towards the van he shouted, 'Look who I've found! We're here! We've made it! Aqaba is relieved!'

The doors of the van flew open and Isabel, Victoria, Ben, Roger and Justin came leaping out into the snow. To Heledd's bewilderment they all looked delighted to see her. They clustered round her all talking at once.

'Thank goodness we've found you!' said Roger. 'Just in time to stop murder being done. Not to mention the radiator boiling dry up that hill.'

'Well, it was your fault. I said we were right,' said Victoria. 'Gosh I'm a good navigator. Aren't you absolutely amazed to see us, Heledd? It's worked out really well, you can guide us to the cottage now.'

'Let's get out of the snow,' said Ben. 'Come up in front with us, Heledd.' He helped her into the van. 'You weren't expecting us, were you?'

Heledd shook her head. Then she remembered a scrap of the conversation Mrs Davies had had with her mother on the phone that morning. She'd been relieved because Mrs Davies had said, 'You're not coming over yourself, then,' in a disapproving voice. After a pause she had said, 'What, in this weather? Well, yes, it will do her good to see them, I daresay. Yes, she's here – come here to the phone, Heledd, and talk to your Mam.' She had taken the receiver from Mrs Davies and said 'Hello, Mam,' but the line was bad and she could not hear what her mother was saying. In the end she had given the receiver back to Mrs Davies and walked away. Then she had felt ashamed of herself for not saying sorry, but she had not had the courage to ask Mrs Davies to let her call her mother back.

'You mustn't worry that you've got to put us all up,' said Roger. 'Iz and Vix are booked into a b and b and we guys have brought camping gear. Mind you, a barn would be welcome.'

'Or we could go and find the Youth Hostel,' said Richard, seeing Heledd's face. 'The only thing is, that road is like a ski run.'

'Well you might look pleased to see us,' said Isabel.

'We're jolly pleased to see you. We've come on a Crusade to find you. We're dying to see your cottage.'

'I am pleased to see you,' said Heledd shyly. 'But it was a shock.' I can't not take them to Craig Wen, she thought. Just to show them. I hope Tristan won't mind. If he's angry, perhaps Mr Davies will let them camp at Tanygraig. Though that might not be easy, with sheep down from the hills for lambing.

'Is there a problem, Heledd?' asked Ben, taking her hand. 'We don't want to impose ourselves if it's not convenient.'

Heledd looked around at her stepsisters and their friends huddled in the camper van, and felt anguish that she could not welcome them proudly and unreservedly to her own hearth as her father would have done.

'It's just that there's someone staying at Craig Wen already,' she said in a rush. 'I don't mean a grown-up. He's only a bit older than us.'

'Heledd, you're blushing! We didn't know you had a boyfriend!'

'He's not a boyfriend!' said Heledd. 'He's just a friend. He was – he needed somewhere to live for a while.'

'Will he let us boil a kettle?' asked Roger, starting up the engine.

'Is it much further, Heledd?' asked Victoria. 'I'm dying for the loo.'

'It's about a mile,' said Heledd. 'It's quite steep,' she told Roger, 'but it's not too snowy yet. Look, there's the turn.'

'Oh glory, it's narrow,' said Roger, leaning tensely over the steering wheel and peering through the windscreen as the wipers swept away the lazily falling snowflakes. 'What if we meet something coming down?'

'We won't, unless the Davieses are going out. That's their turning there. After that the track only goes to Craig Wen. There's a turn-off to the slate quarry but there's nothing down there now except the old workings.' Heledd heard herself jabbering nervously. 'It should be nice and warm in the cottage. Tristan had a good fire going last night,' she said.

'You'll be able to do your prayer mat thing,' said Isabel to Ben. 'Did you know he prays to Allah five times a day?' she told Heledd. 'He's been telling me all about it. And when he still lived in Arabia he used to ride Arab horses. Shall we be able to see your pony, Heleth?'

'Shut up, Iz,' said Victoria. 'One thing at a time. Gosh, I could do with a shower.'

Oh help, thought Heledd. She looked round at Victoria and caught Richard's eye. He must have read her face because he began to laugh. 'No showers, Vix,' he said. 'Isn't that right, Heledd?'

Heledd nodded gratefully.

'No inside loo?'

'No. Just the *tŷ bach*. It means little house,' she explained. 'It's what we call the toilet in Welsh.'

'Oh, Lord, I remember now,' said Victoria. 'Rhiannon said. No running water and no drains either. How did you manage?

'Just as people have managed for centuries,' said Ben. 'You are an over-civilised lot with your flush toilets.'

'See, I told you,' said Justin, nudging Victoria and laughing loudly.

'Shut up, Just,' said Victoria, but she was giggling too.

'Oh well, never mind, you'll just have to have me sweaty.'

The van crawled slowly up the lane and breasted the first rise. Heledd leaned forward and looked through the windscreen towards Craig Wen. There it was, and there was still smoke rising from the chimney. Mr Davies had listened to her, then, and had not driven up there to put Tristan on the train back to Oxford as he had wanted to do.

'There it is,' she said. 'There's Craig Wen.'

'Look at the mountains,' said Richard. 'What a setting. What a place to live. No wonder you didn't want to come to Oxford.'

'It's just like your paintings,' said Victoria. 'They are just so good. You left them out,' she reminded Heledd. 'You don't mind us looking at them, do you?'

'No,' whispered Heledd as the van drew up outside Craig Wen. 'No, I don't mind.'

21

'It's quite all right, Mrs Davies,' said Heledd, speaking on Victoria's mobile phone. 'My s-stepsisters are here with their friends.' She was speaking English for Victoria's benefit, and stumbled over the English for *llyschwiorydd.* 'We are just making a cup of tea. No, I won't be late.' She handed the mobile back to Victoria who disconnected the call.

'Is she making a fuss?' asked Victoria sympathetically.

‘She thinks,’ Heledd began, ‘she thinks I wanted to come back up to Craig Wen because of –’ she broke off in embarrassment.

‘Because of Tristan,’ said Victoria with a grin.

Heledd nodded. They were sitting together on Heledd’s old bed in the *croglofft*, where the mobile could pick up a stronger signal. Downstairs, Tristan was sullenly showing the boys how to fill the boiler.

‘They’re all the same, adults,’ said Victoria. ‘They’ve got sex on the brain. But listen, Heledd, if we’re not welcome, we’ll go. If I thought the only reason Dad and Rhiannon let us come was to spoil things for you and Tristan –’

‘It wasn’t like that,’ said Heledd, agitated. ‘He had nowhere to go, so I gave him the key to Craig Wen. Then when – when I wanted – to come home by myself –’

‘I don’t blame you for taking off,’ said Victoria. ‘We were all pretty hysterical on Friday night, weren’t we?’

‘I forgot he was here,’ whispered Heledd.

‘So Dad and Rhiannon don’t actually know?’

‘They will do by now,’ said Heledd bleakly. ‘Mrs Davies will have told them.’

‘Adults have got such filthy minds,’ said Victoria. ‘I’ve only got to be on my own with Justin for half an hour for somebody to come knocking on the door with some pathetic excuse or other. Mind you, I wouldn’t blame you. I mean, why shouldn’t you have a boyfriend like everyone else? And he’s quite fanciable, Tristan, isn’t he? Sort of wrecked. Justin can be a bit too wholesome, sometimes.’

Isabel’s head appeared at the top of the loft ladder. She was climbing carefully, holding in one hand a jam jar with a string round its neck and a nightlight burning bravely inside. 'I've just been to the little house,' she announced. 'Ben made me a lantern, look!' She placed the jam jar on the floor and stepped up to join them. 'It's snowing like anything!' she said. 'Might we get snowed in?'

'Gosh, I hope so,' said Victoria. 'A week on our own, no parents! We should be so lucky.' She stood up, ducking to avoid the low rafters, and looked out of the tiny gable window. 'Gosh! Look at it!'

'It's snowing a blizzard,' said Roger, climbing up the ladder. 'We ought to be getting you and Iz to the bed and breakfast place, Vix.'

'Out,' said Victoria. 'Get down, Roger, the loft is women's territory. We'll come down and talk about it when we're ready.' She grabbed the end of the ladder and lifted it, forcing Roger to jump hastily to the floor. 'Hey, look! This is really good!'

'Careful!' protested Roger. 'Don't be daft, Vix. If we hang around too long the van'll get stuck.'

'If you think you're going to banish Iz and me to a boring old b and b while the rest of you are camping out here you've got another think coming.'

'Hang on – you're the one who didn't want us to play gooseberry with Tristan and Heledd.'

Heledd said again, 'It's not like that.' She pushed past Victoria and climbed down the ladder into the kitchen. Tristan, Richard and Justin were standing rigidly in front of the kitchen range, glaring at one another. Tristan was holding the empty water bucket as though he had just emptied it over Richard's head. As Richard raised his clenched fist Ben stepped forward and took hold of his wrist.

'Shame, Richard,' he said. 'In a house where you're a guest.'

Richard flushed. Turning, he saw Heledd. 'I'm sorry, Heledd,' he said. 'Sorry,' he said to Tristan. 'I'm out of order. I know we're intruding. We didn't realise.'

'You don't realise nothing, you silly English git,' said Tristan. He thrust the bucket at Richard. 'Get your own effing water. I'm off.'

'No!' cried Heledd.

'Yeah, I'll leave you and your yuppie friends in peace. And good luck to you.'

Victoria leapt down the ladder and confronted Tristan. 'You toe-rag, you'd walk out on her just like that, would you?'

'No!' cried Heledd again. 'You've got it all wrong. Tristan, they've got it all wrong! They think –'

'Pretty obvious what they think!'

'Tell them then! Tell them they're wrong!'

'What the hell do I care what a lot of snotty public school types think? Or you, or your dead bloody father for that matter!' He sat down suddenly and wiped his arm across his face. 'You can all get stuffed. I'm leaving.'

'Oh please!' said Heledd desperately. 'You can't! It's snowing!'

'I know who you are!' exclaimed Victoria suddenly. 'You're the one Dad was talking about. The one who starves himself.'

'They sent him away,' said Heledd when Tristan did not respond. 'From college. Jesus College. They had a name for it.'

'Gosh!' said Richard. 'Were you sent down?'

Tristan took out his asthma inhaler and sucked at it.

'Rusticated,' he muttered after a moment. 'If it's any of your business.'

'Look,' said Roger. 'Never mind all that. We've got to decide what to do. I mean all of us. It's snowing like fury out there. We ought to get Heledd back to the farm and the girls to the guest house while we can.'

'Dream on, Roger,' said Victoria. 'We're staying here. It'll be perfectly all right. Girls upstairs, boys down, not even Ben's parents could object.'

'We've got sleeping bags,' said Richard. 'Not to mention a new cylinder of calor gas – that was your mother's idea, Heledd. And stacks of food. We'll be safer here than anywhere. While the rest of the world is coping with power cuts, here we'll be with our own fire and our own candles, as snug as bugs in rugs. Talk about self-sufficiency. It'll be better than scout camp, duckie.'

'Tell me that again when you have to get up in the middle of the night to dig your way out to the privy, sorry, the what did you call it, Heledd?'

'The little house!' cried Isabel. 'I've been there! It's so sweet, it's got two holes, and ferns growing out of the wall!'

'Golly!' said Victoria to Heledd. 'No wonder you're hardy. I wouldn't mind so much in the snow, but what about when it's pouring with rain?'

'Well,' said Heledd, blushing. Tristan, who had made no move to carry out his threat of leaving, let out a bark of laughter. He stood up and went into the back kitchen, returning a few seconds later with two large, round vessels made of cream china which he plonked down on the table one after the other.

'I've heard that in Oxford they mix the Pimms

Number One in these,' he remarked. 'But round here they come in right handy on a winter's night. A lot better than scout camp, duckie.' He sat down again, rocking his chair back and forth and watching them cynically.

'They've got flowers painted on the inside!' said Isabel. 'Oh, how pretty!' They all laughed. Heledd watched anxiously for Tristan's face to relax.

'Okay, okay,' said Roger. 'We'd better start bringing our stuff in while we can still see what we're doing. Can we do anything about some more light? Does that oil lamp work?'

'Before you light the lamp,' said Tristan, 'you must trim the wick.'

'Oh, right.'

'Otherwise it'll smoke,' said Tristan. 'Ain't that so, girl?'

Heledd nodded. She stood up to deal with the lamp but Ben said, 'You sit by the fire, Heledd. Let me move your chair. Tristan will show us how to light the lamp, won't you, Tristan?'

Tristan shrugged his shoulders. 'If you like.'

An icy wind blew a flurry of snow into the kitchen as the others went outside to unload the camper van. Heledd put another log on the fire, then after a moment's thought went into the little parlour to unpack some tapestry blankets from the oak chest her Aunt Sioned had wanted to sell because she had seen a similar one valued at a huge price on the Antiques Road Show. The blankets felt cold and smelled of mothballs. As she unfolded them Heledd remembered the terrible weekend before Christmas when she and her mother and aunt had packed up the contents of the cottage. Her aunt had never stopped complaining about the inconvenience of not being able to get rid of everything and be done with it.

She would have sent everything to the saleroom if Mam hadn't been there, thought Heledd. She caught her breath to quench a sudden, ridiculous need to weep because she had never shown her gratitude to her mother for not giving in to Aunt Sioned.

'Oh, there you are, Heledd,' said Roger, looking through the doorway. 'Want a hand with those? Where do they go?'

'We used to hang them over the doors and windows,' said Heledd. 'They keep out the wind – the draughts.'

'Right. Oh, by the way, your mother gave me a letter to give to you. I've put it on the mantlepiece, okay?'

Thoughts about her mother were too complicated at the moment. She tried to close her ears to the sound of Victoria upstairs, talking on the mobile phone again. 'We're quite safe – yes, she's here too. Yes, and Tristan, but I don't think – what? sorry, I can't hear you very well – do you want a word? Oh – oh, all right. Yes okay, I'll tell her.'

A moment later she called down, 'Your mum sends her love, Heledd.'

Heledd had climbed onto a stool and was reaching up to hook one of the blankets to the hanging rail above the door.

'She wondered if you'd read her letter yet. She says to phone her whenever you feel like it.' She watched Heledd curiously as she stepped down from the stool. 'She sounded a bit pecular,' she said.

Roger had put the letter on the high shelf above the kitchen range, propped behind another of Ben's jam jar lanterns. Heledd's name, written on the envelope in her mother's flowing handwriting, jumped in the candlelight.

'Ugh, it's cold!' shouted Isabel, rushing into the kitchen. 'Can we make some toast in front of the fire, Heleth? With a toasting fork?'

'Heledd, what am I doing wrong?' asked Ben from behind the smoking paraffin lamp.

I'll read the letter later, thought Heldd. There's too much to do at the moment. With relief, she turned her attention to the practical business of organising the household, just as she had always done.

22

I'll read the letter tomorrow, thought Heldd as she sat with the others round the fire after a supper of jacket potatoes and baked beans with cheese grated over the top. Isabel sat on the stool, leaning against Heledd's legs in a sisterly sort of way which Heledd found surprisingly comfortable. Victoria and Justin were entwined in the single armchair, and Richard, Roger and Ben had pulled up kitchen chairs. Even Tristan was there, sitting cross-legged on the rag rug, peeling an orange and tossing the bits of peel into the fire.

'We should be telling sad stories of the death of kings,' said Richard. 'Or reciting ballads and sagas while the wolves howl outside. Tell us a story, Heledd. Tell us how you met Tristan – no, I know! Read us the poem you were telling us about. The one about Lawrence.'

Heledd looked across at Tristan. Last night she had offered to leave the poem for him to re-read, but he had thrust it wordlessly back into her suitcase and slammed down the lid while Mr Davies looked on suspiciously.

'You said you'd translate it for us,' said Richard.

Heledd said evasively, 'I forgot.'

'Never mind, let's have the other one about the court being dark tonight. I love it, it makes me feel as though I've lived a thousand years.'

'For Pete's sake, Rich, leave the poor girl alone,' said Victoria. 'It's half term. We're supposed to be on holiday. Mind you, I should be revising,' she added with a sigh, slumping back against Justin's shoulder.

'What's the chances of doing some climbing?' asked Justin. 'I've never been up Snowdon in the winter.'

'Whatever else we do,' said Richard, 'we're going to visit Lawrence of Arabia's birthplace. I've been looking at the map, it'll be a wonderful scenic drive.'

'We'll have to dig our way out before we can do anything,' said Roger, getting up and peering behind the tapestry blanket that was draped over the kitchen window. 'It's still snowing.'

'Funny how quiet it is,' said Justin. 'There's not even any wind.'

'No parents, no teachers, no hassle,' said Victoria. 'Bliss. No Creepy Christopher putting his hand on my bum. Triple bliss.'

'You're kidding,' said Justin after a moment's silence.

'It was only once,' said Victoria. 'I booted him in the shin and he gave me a twenty pound note not to tell Mum. I stood there in front of him and tore it into little pieces. Boy did I enjoy doing that. But once was enough, thank you very much. For God's sake, don't say anything to Dad,' she added, glaring fiercely round at all of them. 'He would go quadruple ballistic.'

'I knew Creepy Christopher was horrible!' cried Isabel. 'Oh I do wish Mum would get a new boyfriend. I'm never going there again!'

'It was only once,' said Victoria again. 'Don't worry, Iz, he was only trying it on. I shouldn't have mentioned it. Let's talk about something else. Tell us how you met Tristan, Heledd.'

Heledd looked doubtfully at Tristan but he just shrugged as he picked shreds of pith off a segment of orange.

'It was up a tower,' she said.

'St. Mary's,' said Tristan. 'They'll know the one.'

'I was climbing the tower,' said Heledd. 'I was climbing the tower and there he was. He'd been there all night, he must have been because the ticket lady said I was the first that day.'

'Why?' asked Victoria. 'You must have been frozen.'

'I dunno,' said Tristan. 'I just felt like it. Her Dad did it once.' He jerked his head in Heledd's direction.

'It's the kind of stupid thing you do,' said Roger to Richard. 'I bet he breaks the ice to swim in the Cherwell too.'

'Shut up,' said Richard. 'Sometimes it's important.'

''Strewth!' said Justin from beneath Victoria's mane of hair. 'Sometimes you're barmy!'

'Infantile,' said Roger.

'But it doesn't freeze over like it used to,' said Richard.

'Fortunately,' said Tristan.

'What on earth are you two on about?' asked Victoria.

'Do you know about her Dad?' Tristan continued, ignoring Victoria. 'And that telly mast he climbed up? When he came down he was covered in ice and he was lucky not to lose his fingers and toes from frostbite. He practised for that by climbing towers and swimming in the Cherwell in winter because he'd read that's what Lawrence of Arabia did to harden himself up before going off to free the Arabs, ha, ha.' He threw a piece of orange peel at Richard. 'What a joke. What a waste of time.'

'Another dreamer of the day,' murmured Ben.

Richard said, 'I know that's what some people think about Lawrence of Arabia, but is that what you think about Heledd's Dad?'

'Yes,' said Tristan, catching Heledd's eye. 'No. I don't know. Who cares anyway? Sooner or later we're all dead.'

'Or middle managers,' said Justin.

'I wish I cared enough about my language to climb up television masts,' said Richard. 'I bet you would, Ben, wouldn't you?'

'Oh yes,' said Ben seriously. 'If I thought I could never read the Holy Koran in Arabic again I would climb up a great many television masts, I assure you.'

'He means it, you see. The rest of us just strike attitudes,' said Richard to Tristan.

'Vanity, that's all it is,' said Tristan. 'And it'll probably kill him too.'

That's in the poem, thought Heledd, with anguish. That's what Dad was writing about in the poem.

Tristan gave a long sniff and stuffed another orange

segment into his mouth. He saw her watching him and looked away. 'You an Arab, then, are you?' he asked Ben.

'Yes, I was born in Damascus.'

'So what's your opinion of the sainted Lawrence?'

'Don't ask!' said Richard.

'Oh glory,' said Victoria. 'Give over about Lawrence of flaming Arabia. It was a good film, all right? The best bit was Omar Sharif on his camel, riding up out of the desert.'

'All those black tassels,' said Richard. 'Divine.'

'Gosh, it's cold up here,' said Victoria, as they prepared for bed several hours later. 'Was it such a good idea to leave the boys downstairs, I ask myself? Good thing we remembered hot water bottles. We'll have to cuddle up together to keep warm. Put a sweater on over your jim-jams, Iz, that'll help.'

'We must keep the fire in the parlour going,' said Heledd. 'It helps to warm the loft.'

'It's not bad, really,' said Victoria. '*En suite* chamber pot and all.' They had hung a blanket over the old wooden clothes horse to screen off a corner of the loft, for privacy. 'Goodnight, boys!' she called downstairs. 'Sleep well!'

'Heledd!' called Roger. 'Don't forget your letter!'

'Oh – thank you.'

'Shall I pass it up to you?'

'Oh – no, no. I'll read it tomorrow.'

'Okay. Goodnight, then.'

'Goodnight.'

23

Have I slept or not? wondered Heledd, opening her eyes early the following morning and slowly realising that she was no longer squashed on the bed with Victoria and Isabel but tangled up in a strange sleeping bag on the floor. But it was definitely her Craig Wen rug she was lying on, and those were definitely the Craig Wen rafters with their flaking whitewash above her head.

So she really was at home. She wasn't just dreaming.

The house breathed gently with sleeping people. Victoria and Isabel were totally hidden under sleeping bags and quilts. Heledd sat up quietly and looked about her. Daylight was filtering through the thin bedroom curtain her mother had contrived, years ago, from an old chenille tablecloth. Stealthily she felt for her trousers and sweater and pulled them on over her pyjamas, then put on her socks and trainers and crept carefully to the window and drew the curtain aside. She wiped away the condensation from the glass and looked out at a luminous white landscape under a low grey sky. Snow had drifted deeply round the byre, and hung on the branches of the elder tree. Below the window she could see the camper van, marooned in snow to the top of its wheels.

She tiptoed to the ladder and climbed down into the shadowy kitchen. There was still a residue of warmth from the fire. She passed the box bed inside which she could hear Tristan's chesty breathing, and went out to the back kitchen to look for kindling and matches to get the fire going again. Seeing with surprise that the back door was slightly ajar, she opened it wide and looked outside.

She was not the first one up after all. A line of deep footprints crossed the yard towards the stream, which cut a glinting pewter channel through the snow as it tumbled down its rocky gully. Ben, dressed only in jeans and a pyjama jacket, was leaning over the snowy bank of the stream letting the water run over his hands. He cupped water in his hands and splashed it over his head, and Heledd heard him gasp quietly at the cold of it. Then he stood up, and she saw that he had trodden down a patch of snow nearby and had laid out his prayer mat.

You could see the sea from this side of the house but Ben was facing the other way, towards the dawn. Heledd watched him step onto the mat, then bow, kneel and bend forward until his forehead touched the bright crimson pile. There was something deeply reverent and beautiful about the way he prayed. Heledd could not help but watch. She felt ashamed because it had not occurred to her to say any prayers, not once since she had left Oxford. Not proper prayers. I'm sorry, she apologised to God. I'm sorry I forgot to thank you for bringing me home. Then she added, and thank you for bringing Iz and Vix and the boys here too, and for not letting Tristan leave just yet.

'Good morning!' Ben was smiling as he paddled through the snow back to the house, his prayer mat rolled up under his arm.

'I didn't mean to stare,' said Heledd shyly.

'The light!' said Ben. 'The sea! It's wonderful! The mountains!'

'You must be cold,' said Heledd. 'I was just going to get the fire going.'

'Let me help. Is there more wood?'

He helped her to collect a basketful of logs from the byre, and she found a few dry twigs and a firelighter. She lit the fire while Ben drew back the quilt that was covering the kitchen window, and went out to the spring to fill the kettle. Presently the fire was leaping into life, and they pulled up chairs and sat watching the flames dart up the chimney.

'That's better,' said Ben, leaning forward and holding his hands out to the fire. 'I hope Allah took note of how very cold the water was just now!'

'Well, your angels probably did,' said Heledd.

Ben laughed. 'Don't tell me you've done a project on Islam too?'

'Oh no,' said Heledd. 'But I know about the angels. My father told me.'

'Keeping an eye on us!' said Ben. 'Keeping an eye on me now as I do the forbidden thing, sit alone with a person of the opposite sex. My mother and father have great faith in my angels.'

'Isn't it allowed?' Heledd tried to remember other things her father had told her about what Moslems believed. Pictures of women completely covered in black robes, with only their eyes showing, came to mind.

'Very strict Moslems –' Ben broke off, and sighed. 'Well, my parents are pretty liberal really. I wouldn't be at a mixed school like TEL if they weren't. I wouldn't be here either.' He hesitated, then continued, 'My mother didn't really want me to come, but she didn't forbid me.'

His troubled expression hinted at deeper, more painful conflicts, but all he said was, 'I can't divide myself off from my friends, whatever their sex. Or their religion, or their nationality.' He looked around the kitchen at the whitewashed stone walls and painted cupboards. 'In our house in Damascus the beams were painted blue,' he said. 'Pale blue. And from the roof you could see the Umayyad Mosque.'

'And you had myrtle bushes in the garden,' said Heledd. She wanted to add something about how sad it was that he could never go back, but shyness overcame her. Instead she sat up and looked around the kitchen which was still littered with dirty plates and food containers from the night before.

'Let me help you clear up,' said Ben. 'What a mess we left last night!'

'Oh no, really, you mustn't. You're a guest.' She got to her feet. The routine at Craig Wen had always been mornings for chores: filling the boiler, milking, feeding the animals, food preparation; and afternoons for reading, writing and painting. There was no reason why things should not be done the same way now. If she began at once she could do most of the cleaning up while the others were still in bed out of the way, and if there were eggs and flour in that box of groceries her mother had sent she might even manage to make a batch of *crempog* for breakfast.

24

'We'd better get digging,' said Roger, later that morning after they had all surfaced and eaten their fill of pancakes.

'What for?' asked Victoria. 'We shan't be going anywhere.'

'Well, we need to be able to get to the little house, to start with.'

'Not to mention disposing of the Pimms No 1,' said Richard, licking jam off his knife. 'You'll need to instruct us, Heledd.'

There was no point in being delicate. 'It all goes on the midden,' said Heledd. 'Then you dig some soil over, or straw from cleaning out the animals.'

'And what about when there aren't any animals, and the midden is under a foot of snow?'

'The snow usually melts,' said Heledd, blushing. 'It's quite warm, you see.'

Victoria wrinkled her nose. 'What a thing to have to tell us about!'

'It doesn't smell,' Heledd assured her. 'Dad built a special wall round it to keep it tidy.'

'We'll just have to get it going again,' said Roger. 'Okay, folks, to work! Whatever snow-shifting tools we can find.'

'All right, Scoutmaster, we're on our way.'

While the Oxford party was clearing the snow Heledd made a tour of inspection of the house and the outbuildings, checking for storm damage or evidence of rats. She looked at the log pile and calculated that it would last quite a few more days yet. She counted the remaining few bales of hay in the barn. Then she went indoors and loaded the groceries her mother had sent into the old freezer where the food would be safe from rats and mice.

The kitchen was looking more like its old self every moment. Heledd opened cupboards and boxes, setting out saucepans and plates and cutlery and mugs on the table next to the sink. Then she opened another box and felt a rush of joy as she came across some of her father's books. They included *Seven Pillars of Wisdom,* the precious Gregynog Press book *The Stealing of the Mare* with its Art Deco cover, a number of Loeb Classics with their red and green bindings, and a paperback edition of *Ariel*, the biography of Shelley by André Maurois. Finally there were some Welsh poetry and novels and a proof copy of one of her father's books.

Tristan sat by the fire watching her as she arranged the books on the shelves her father had built in the alcove by the chimney. He had taken off his trainers and Heledd could not help seeing that the soles were coming away from the uppers. After a moment's thought she went into the back kitchen and looked inside the old cupboard where her father always used to keep his climbing boots. They were still there – Aunt Sioned must have overlooked them or she would certainly have thrown them away. They were dry and cracked and full of cobwebs but the stitching was sound and the soles were thick, and a good oiling would soon soften them up.

She dusted off the worst of the cobwebs and took the boots into the other room. Tristan was standing by the shelves looking at the books Heledd had just put out. He had taken one of them down and was reading it. When

Heledd spoke he pushed it hurriedly back onto the shelf and turned defensively.

'Do you think these might fit you?' she asked. 'If they're too big, I'll see if I can find some socks.'

Tristan looked at the boots. Without saying anything, he sat down by the fire again. Heledd put the boots down on the rug by his feet and left him to it. She put her own boots on, and her duffel coat, and went outside to see how the others were getting on.

Their bright jackets and knitted hats were a colourful sight against the dazzling snow. Their cheeks were flushed with the cold.

'We should have brought skis!' called Victoria, waving to her. 'It's like Switzerland!'

'Better,' said Roger. 'You can't see the sea in Switzerland. Heledd, come and tell us what these mountains are.'

'There's a better view, if we climb up a bit,' she replied. 'If we can get onto the rock above the spring.' She stepped cautiously into an unspoiled patch of the soft snow and they floundered after her. Five minutes later they were standing on the knoll above Craig Wen, looking down the snow-filled valley towards the sea. The snow had blotted out all the features of the landscape, except for the occasional tree. It was like looking out over a rolling white desert, with craggy mountains in the background.

'It's a white-out!' said Isabel. 'You can't see anything except snow! Not a single house!'

'Only pylons,' said Victoria, looking at the power lines that looped across the middle distance.

'Which way is Snowdon?'

Heledd gestured towards the south west. 'You have to go higher to see it from here,' she said. 'All sorts of places are hidden when you look from this point. Bangor's down there, and Bethesda's that way, and all those hills over there are where the slate quarries are, and Dinorwic and Deiniolen. They're places, I mean towns, not mountains,' she added.

'Those are the Carnedds!' said Justin, who was looking in a different direction.

'Yes!' Heledd turned to him with a pleased smile, then pointed to the distant peaks in turn. 'Carnedd Dafydd, and Carnedd Llewelyn.'

'I bet you've been up both of them.'

'Oh yes, Dad and I go up – I mean we used to go up every year. You can walk in a big circle and come back by Bera Bach and Y Drosgl. It's best in winter.'

'You'd never do it in this weather, Heledd?' Victoria sounded amazed.

'Well, perhaps not while there's quite so much snow –'

As she was speaking, Heledd saw movement a few hundred yards away across the moorland. 'Shush!' she said to the others. 'Shush! Look, Isabel!'

She pointed. A small herd of shaggy ponies, each with a thick duvet of snow on its back, had wandered into view, hooves pawing and noses pushing through the snow to find grazing. They caught the scent of the humans and lifted their heads warily, ears pricked.

'Ponies!' breathed Isabel. 'Wild ponies!'

'Rhiannon, there are ponies,' gabbled Isabel on the mobile phone, the moment they got back to the house.

'There are real wild ponies. This is the best place I've ever been to in my whole life.'

'We must put some bales of hay out for them before it gets dark,' said Heledd.

'We'll do that, Heledd, just say the word,' said Roger.

'And we're going to put hay out for them,' Isabel told Rhiannon. 'And we had pancakes for breakfast that Helly made on a sort of flat frying pan. We had them with jam. And we climb up the ladder to bed, just like you said. Yes, she's here now. Shall I put you on?' She held out the phone, and Heledd could not avoid taking it.

'Heledd, *cariad*,' said her mother. '*Popeth yn iawn*? Everything all right?'

Heledd struggled to speak. 'Y-yes, yes thank you.'

'Is there much snow?'

'Yes – yes, it's quite deep.'

'They're forecasting frost tonight, but a thaw in a day or two,' said her mother. 'So you shouldn't be cut off for long. What's the food situation?'

'We've got plenty of food, thank you. Vix – Victoria's making lasagne for lunch.'

'Tell her I'm putting that vegetarian haggis in it!' shouted Victoria, opening a tin of tomatoes at the kitchen table. 'The only thing we haven't got are the brussels sprouts!'

It wasn't too difficult, talking to her mother about practicalities, but it wasn't enough. All the other things heaved under the surface. Her mother sounded strangely nervous. Heledd rang off, feeling cowardly, and turned to see if Tristan had tried on the boots yet. He was still sitting by the fire, his feet black and bare. He was reading a book with close attention. Heledd scurried up the ladder to look for a pair of her father's socks for him. As she came down she heard Richard ask, 'What's that you're reading?'

Tristan began to read aloud from the book, but it seemed to be in no language any of them had ever heard before. A sing-song language with unexpected stresses. After a few moments he broke off, smirking up at Richard and sucking his teeth.

'What *is* that?' Richard leaned forward to pull the book out of Tristan's hand but he snatched it out of reach. 'It's not Latin!'

'It is *The Odyssey* of Homer,' said Ben. 'He is reading from the Greek.'

'Greek!' said Richard. 'How come you know Greek? I know where he gets it from,' he added, jerking a thumb at Ben. 'His Dad. But you?'

'No, it ain't exactly what they teach in comprehensives in Swansea, I suppose,' said Tristan.

'That's my father's book,' said Heledd. 'He studied Greek at Oxford. And Latin. They had a special name for it. *Literae* something.'

'Greats!' said Roger. 'Did he read Greats? Blimey, he must have been –' he turned on Tristan. 'Is that what you're reading? Greats?'

'I doubt it, any longer,' said Tristan. 'But that was the original intention, yes. Doing Mods this year. Dead languages, passport to the new millennium, I don't think.' He sniffed, closed the book and handed it casually to Richard. Bending forward, he picked up one of Rheinallt's boots and thrust his bare foot into it.

'I got you some socks,' said Heledd hastily. He took

them without looking at her and put them on. She and the boys watched him expectantly but he did not look up.

'What I want to know,' said Richard, 'is how anybody knows how Classical Greek is pronounced. I mean, they didn't leave tapes, did they?'

'Mind out, you lot, I want to get to the oven,' Victoria sang out, elbowing her way round the boys, the tray of lasagne in her hands. Heledd grabbed a tea towel and opened the range oven door for her, then put another log on the fire.

'I tell you what,' said Victoria. 'We should be on telly doing all this Victorian kitchen cookery. I didn't know I had it in me.'

'You'd hardly be cooking lasagne in a Victorian kitchen,' said Roger.

'Whaddyou mean? I've just done that very thing. It'll be at least three quarters of an hour yet, though. Anyone want some peanuts? Coke?'

'In a bit,' said Roger. 'Let's put this hay out first. What do we do, Heledd?'

'If we carry a bale to the far side of the barn where it's sheltered, and then break it up,' said Heledd, 'the ponies will probably come down for it. If we carry it up onto the hill it'll just blow away or sink into a bog or something.'

'Right you are. Are you coming, Iz?'

Outside, the cloud had thinned and the afternoon sun was casting long pink rays across the landscape. 'It's going to be really cold tonight,' said Roger as they went into the barn. 'But will it snow again, I wonder?'

'I hope so,' said Isabel. 'I want to stay here for ever and ever. They'll have to drop food parcels from helicopters. Oh!' She jumped and squealed as they moved a hay bale and a mouse dashed out between her feet.

'It's only a mouse,' said Heledd.

'I'm not frightened,' said Isabel. 'I just didn't want to tread on it. What's mouse in Welsh?'

'*Llygoden,*' said Heledd.

'Cl-cluggodden. Did I say it right?'

'Very good,' said Heledd. *'Da iawn.'*

'Well, that was delicious, though I say it myself,' said Victoria. 'And as I did all the cooking you lot can do all the washing up. What I'm going to do now is sit by the fire and read a book. What have you got, Heledd?' She pranced across the room and frowned at the two shelves of books Heledd had unpacked that morning. 'U – oh, I suppose they're all in Welsh.'

'Or Greek,' said Richard.

'Gosh, look at this!' said Victoria, taking down the Gregynog Press book. 'What a fabulous book. Look at this fantastic picture, Iz! *The Celebrated Romance of the Stealing of the Mare*,' she read aloud. 'Gosh, listen, Ben, it says, translated from the original Arabic by Lady Anne Blunt.'

'Let me see!' Ben took the book, turning the creamy vellum pages reverently. 'How beautiful! How did your father come to own such a book, Heledd?'

'It was printed in Wales,' said Heledd. 'I think it belonged to his father.'

'Hello, this one's in English,' said Victoria, taking down a paperback novel entitled *Feet in Chains*. 'Have you read it, Heledd?'

'It's called *Traed Mewn Cyffion* in Welsh,' said Heledd. 'Kate Roberts is a famous writer in Wales. She wrote about people working on the farms and in the quarries.' The English translation had been sent to her father for review, and he kept it alongside the original to lend to people who didn't speak Welsh, because he said it was a world masterpiece and ought to be better known.

'The farm in the story is a bit like Craig Wen,' explained Heledd. 'The families who lived here farmed, but the men worked in the quarries too. They worked in our quarry here or they walked to the Penrhyn quarries the other side of Bethesda.'

Tristan looked up suddenly from the Loeb Homer. 'And were they strikers or blacklegs in the Penrhyn lock-outs in 1903?'

'I – I don't know,' said Heledd, startled.

'My Nain used to say that when she was a kid in school they'd still call kids from the families who went back to work *bradwyr*, traitors, even in the nineteen-thirties,' said Tristan.

'Your Nain! Was she from these parts then?'

Tristan nodded off-handedly, 'Oh yeah, she was a Gog, like you.'

'A what?' said Justin, Richard and Roger together.

'He means I'm a North Walian,' explained Heledd. 'It comes from *y gogledd* which means the north. But where was your Nain from? What was her name?' she asked Tristan.

'You wouldn't have known her,' said Tristan.

'I'd be interested to see a slate quarry,' said Roger. 'Heledd, do you say there's one near here?'

'Yes. It's not been worked for years. You can still see

the workings, though, and the ruins of the *caban* where the men used to take their breaks.'

'Can we get to it? I'd love to have a look.'

'Well – it's quite an easy walk, usually, but the snow's awfully deep for walking far.'

'It won't be so bad tomorrow. We'll have to do something, we can't stay indoors all week no matter what the weather's like.'

'Speak for yourself,' said Victoria, flopping into the armchair and opening *Feet in Chains.*

25

The next morning the surface of the snow was frozen to a crust and the edge of the stream glittered with icicles, but Ben still went out before the sun came up to wash and pray. Heledd watched from the kitchen door, waiting for him to finish before stepping outside to fill the kettle. As he rose from his knees he waved and smiled. Returning his wave she realised she was not alone: Richard and Roger were standing behind her.

'And you think you're tough,' Roger said to Richard.

In reply Richard pulled off his sweatshirt and thrust it at his brother. 'We could all do with a wash,' he said. 'I don't mind going first. Excuse us, Heledd.'

He ran barefoot across the yard to the spring and ducked his head under the trickle of water, shouting with the shock of the cold. He scooped the water over his arms and back and scooped handfuls of snow to rub on his slender white chest. Then he ran back to the house, leaping and skidding over the snow and laughing wildly. He grabbed his sweatshirt from Roger and used it to rub himself dry. 'Oh wow! Oh wow!' he cried, hopping from one foot to the other as he dried his feet. 'Fantastic!'

'Get dressed, you lunatic,' said Roger, throwing a towel at him. 'Get him a dry sweater, would you, Ben? And some socks – his feet are blue.'

'It's wonderful,' said Richard between chattering teeth. 'You must do it.'

'Not on your life,' said Roger. 'With Heledd's permission I'll heat some water and have a civilised wash in the parlour. Then we'll take ourselves off for a bit so that the girls can do the same.'

'I'm glad I did it,' said Richard to Ben. 'I don't care what he says.'

'But I didn't see you pray,' said Ben gently.

Poor Richard, thought Heledd impulsively, seeing his triumphant expression change to one of startled shame. After a moment he said, 'I didn't do it to mock or blaspheme, Ben.'

'I know.' Ben took Richard's hand quickly, then released it.

'Anyway I do pray. Not quite sure who to, but I do pray. All the time. For you, for me, for Roger, for all of us.'

'Breakfast,' interrupted Roger, rolling his eyes at Heledd. 'Get dressed, for crying out loud,' he said to Richard. 'And then you can fill the boiler, as you're feeling so fit. I'll bring some more logs in.'

Roger was still in scoutmaster mode as he doled out porridge at breakfast. 'We ought to see if we can get down to the village,' he said. 'See if the bottom road's passable. We could do with some fresh milk. Is there a shop, Heledd?'

'We could get milk from Tanygraig,' said Heledd, reluctant to think about having to face the Davieses.

'Is that the farm where your pony lives now?' asked Isabel. 'Can we go and see her?'

It would certainly be easier with Isabel. Even so she said, 'It's quite a long way to walk in this much snow. If we wait until tomorrow it may be clearer.'

'Besides, Iz, we ought to have a bath,' said Victoria. 'And if we pack the boys off to find the shop we can do it in front of the fire. This means you too, Tristan.'

'I'll get you one of Dad's sweaters,' said Heledd quickly, as Tristan pulled a face.

'He won't need it, if he's used to sleeping out on St. Mary's Tower,' said Richard provocatively, but Tristan only grinned round his mouthful of toast.

At mid-day, as the grey sky lowered and the mist crept down the mountains, Richard, Ben and Tristan stood on a high rock looking down at the shattered workings of the Craig Wen quarry. The snow had blown off the spoil heaps and the exposed faces of the slate terraces, but had drifted deeply round the ruined stone buildings and abandoned lifting gear on the quarry floor.

'God, this is an awful place,' said Richard.

'There's been a new rock fall,' said Tristan, pointing at a pale grey river of scree on the far side of the quarry. 'That'll have been the frost. But look, you can see where they got the good slate from. They had to get it in good clean blocks, then they'd take it down to the sheds to be split.'

'Imagine the dust! It must have been as bad as a coal mine!'

'Worse,' said Tristan. 'They died young, the quarrymen. See that?' He pointed to a bent stalk of iron fencing that stuck out over the edge of the quarry. 'That'll be what's left of the steps they used to get down to the terraces. Up and down god knows how many steps and that was on top of the five mile walk to work. I tell you, we don't know the half.'

'You seem to know,' said Ben, peering down into the quarry with a shudder.

'Yeah,' said Tristan. After a pause he added, 'My Taid – my grandfather – worked in the quarries. Not this one – Dinorwic, he worked. This is a piddling little quarry compared to Dinorwic. He was what they called a rockman. He was killed in an explosion. Killed by a charge of his own dynamite, they said.' He grinned sideways at the other two boys. 'I've often wondered if old Lawrence had Welsh quarrymen with him in the desert when they were dynamiting the railways.'

'Gosh,' said Richard. 'Lawrence loved explosions. Perhaps it's all because he heard them in his pram at Tremadog. Subliminal, you know.'

Their laughter rang eerily round the quarry. A patch of snow slid out of a crack in the rock and slithered down in a small avalanche, billowing up like spume on the sea as it hit the quarry floor. The boys backed hurriedly from the cliff edge.

'Imagine working in these conditions year in, year out,' said Richard. 'It makes one feel such a wimp in comparison.'

'They didn't let it get them down,' said Tristan. 'They had debates and talks and committee meetings in their breaks. They were big on chapel and education. My grandfather taught himself to read Latin and Greek.'

'Ah!' said Ben. 'Did he teach you?'

'No, he died years ago, when my Mam was little. My Nain gave me his books, though.'

'We're so pathetic,' said Richard. 'All we do is play at being brave and tough. What's the point? Even my father. He's making a documentary in Tashkent. If he ran into any trouble, the BBC would just fly him out. He couldn't split a slate to save his life. I'm jumping naked in the snow to impress Ben. Why aren't I doing something with some point to it?' He snatched off his Arab head cloth and threw it into the quarry.

'Richard,' said Ben. 'Do shut up.'

'How Heledd must despise us,' said Richard. 'Her father was a real man of action.' He turned on his heel and began to tramp through the snow up the steep track down which they had slid half an hour before.

'What's the matter with him?' asked Tristan. 'He'd have been splitting slate all right, if it was the only way to earn a living. He wants to be thankful, the silly bugger. Sorry,' he added. 'I know he's your boyfriend and all that.'

'He's my close friend,' said Ben. 'That's all.'

'I see,' said Tristan. 'He's gay, you're not. Unfortunate.'

'Richard's not gay,' said Ben, digging his hands into his pockets. 'You English are obsessed with people being gay.'

‘Yurr,’ said Tristan in his most South Walian accent. ‘Do you mind? Call me what you like, but don’t call me English.’

‘Sorry,’ said Ben. ‘I forgot. You sound different from Heledd, you see.’

‘More of a hybrid, me,’ said Tristan. ‘There’s more English spoken in Swansea than there is in Bethesda, for a start.’

‘But your parents were Welsh-speaking?’

‘I never heard my Mam speak a word of Welsh,’ said Tristan.

‘But you speak it,’ said Ben.

Tristan smiled grimly at Ben’s baffled expression. ‘Oh yes, my Nain saw to that.’

‘What about your father?’

‘Who knows?’ said Tristan. ‘Not a chap I ever met. Come on, let’s get after Lawrence of Arabia.’

They caught Richard up at the top of the track where he stood looking down towards the mist-shrouded coast, his fair hair blowing in the soft, thawing wind. He grinned sheepishly as they joined him, and they made their way laboriously back to the cottage.

‘Post!’ said Roger, as he and Justin tramped into the kitchen at Craig Wen shortly after the other boys. ‘Milk! Bread! Choccy biccies! There’s not nearly so much snow in the village,’ he said. ‘I tell you what, the people in the post office, their eyes were shooting out of their heads when we walked in. They were terribly polite: it was quite unnerving.’

'They thought we were hippies, you could tell,' said Justin.

'Well, it's what you look like at the moment. I said you should have washed your hair,' said Victoria, sorting through the bundle of letters. 'Hullo, there's a letter for you, Tristan. The rest are for – oh dear, Heledd's Dad, I suppose.'

'Can't be for me,' said Tristan. 'Nobody knows I'm here.' He frowned at the handwriting on the envelope, then carried it away into the box bed. Heledd took the remaining letters. They were mostly circulars, but there were two largeish envelopes addressed to her, their postmarks obliterated by the damp after weeks in the post box at the bottom of the lane. Opening them she found condolence cards from two of her old school teachers. She read them several times, brooding over them as though waiting for more words to emerge on the page alongside the mass-produced message and signature. It had given her a shock to receive mail addressed to her here, at home, at Craig Wen. It was a pity that the contents were such a disappointment.

But it was her own fault. She hadn't kept in touch with any of her local friends. Not that she'd had many. Her father had always been the most important person in her life.

She put the cards back into their envelopes, suppressing a chilly fear that staying on permanently at Craig Wen might not be the right thing to do after all. She might not be wanted.

Don't! she rebuked herself. It was too soon to give up yet. She hadn't made any plans, or done any of the things she had meant to, like going into Bethesda to look for a job. She had been too busy with visitors. It would be easier at the end of the week, when they had gone. Not that she wouldn't miss them, even if they did speak English all the time so that she couldn't hear herself think.

They can all come and visit me whenever they want, she told herself. But Craig Wen isn't just for holidays, it's for life. She shuddered to think of what people like Iwan Davies Tanygraig would do if they thought Craig Wen was being used as a holiday home.

'I'm sorry to have missed the quarry,' said Roger as they ate bread and cheese and apples for lunch. 'Can we go again this afternoon?'

'If we take some ropes and stuff we can abseil down to the bottom,' suggested Justin. 'Quarries can be good for climbing.'

'We're coming too,' said Victoria. 'How about it, girls? It's not nearly as cold.'

It proved quite easy to avoid being included in the party. Heledd felt grateful to Roger and Victoria for seeming to realise that she would like some time to herself. After they had set off, taking a reluctant Tristan with them, she wandered around the house for a while, trying to retrieve the sense of being safe at home that she associated with her life here with her father. She tidied up, folding discarded sweaters and towels and shaking the table-cloth. She opened both the outside doors to let some fresh air blow away the smell of unwashed bodies, and put some more logs on the fire. But the old feeling would not come back. It was as though both she and the house were anxiously waiting for the others to return.

To conquer her unease she climbed to the loft and took out her father's last poem from her suitcase. It would be good for her to have another go at understanding it. She felt that if only she could fathom what her father was trying to say, she might know what he wanted her to do.

But all this business about feet of sand, she didn't understand it. The English talked about feet of clay, and he seemed to have turned them into sand because of Lawrence of Arabia and the desert. Except that he seemed to be talking about his own feet of sand, and he used some strange Latin words in the middle of the Welsh. He seemed to be accusing himself of something, as though he were guilty of some terrible crime which he could never confess. Then there was the dedication, and that was the most difficult matter of all. *I Rhiannon*. Not Heledd, his daughter, but Rhiannon, his wife, who had betrayed him.

It was no good. Heledd folded up the worn sheets of lined paper and put them back in their envelope. Her fingers touched her father's last letter, but she did not take it out to re-read. She knew it by heart. *Trust your mother*, he had written. If only she could. Perhaps her mother would understand the poem. Perhaps he wanted her to give it to her mother. That was a difficult thought.

She looked round the kitchen. Her mother's letter was still on the mantlepiece, propped behind the jam jar lantern where Roger had left it for her.

She didn't want to read it. She didn't want to think about it or about the poem any more. She put the kettle on the fire and made herself a cup of instant coffee. Looking at her watch, she saw it was not yet three. She went outside to look for the others but saw no sign of them. Finally, as off-handedly as she could manage, she took down the envelope and pushed her thumb under the flap.

26

Oxford, Sunday

Dearest Heledd,

I am so relieved to hear that you have arrived safely – I expect the Davieses told you that they had asked Iwan to meet you off the train as they were visiting Mrs Davies's mother in Pwllheli – but then Iwan became engrossed in surfing the net and forgot all about it, and of course it blocked their phone line so we couldn't get through. None of us knew that you were travelling with a friend.

Darling, I've heard many worrying things about Tristan, but I can understand that you feel the two of you have a lot in common – you've both lost a parent, and I hear he's as full of Welsh poetry as your father was. I also have to say that when your father was an undergraduate he was just as unwashed as David tells me Tristan is. But please, darling, do take care. Don't get involved too deeply. Remember that you aren't sixteen yet and Tristan could get into trouble with the law.

Oh dear, so much of what I hear about Tristan reminds me of your father. Going without food or sleep for days just to prove that he could; sleeping on the Jesus Chapel roof in the middle of winter – completely idiotic but completely loveable at the same time. I suppose all those endurance tests he inflicted on himself stood him in good stead during the language campaign but I know they destroyed his constitution and probably killed him in the end. I can feel my old anger surging through me as I write – but I must respect what he did. Nothing they tried to imply about him when he was arrested for conspiracy was true. He was completely open and honest, he had no spite or envy. He was the best friend in the world to me when I ended my first affair with David. He was the only person who didn't keep telling me that David was just having a fling with a student. He stood by me when no one else did, not even my parents. He loved me so much, I could not help but love him in return. Probably I should not have married him, but then we should not have had you, Heledd, and I will never forget the look of joy on your father's face when he first saw you. Nor do I want to forget the happy, happy times we had together when you were little.

Darling, there's so much of my life I need to share with you, and there are things I should have explained to you years ago. But I was afraid – and anyway it seemed unfair to both you and Rheinallt, when I truly believed, as I did for many years, that I had put David behind me.

I'm so sorry, my darling, this is turning into a terrible ramble of a letter. Probably I shouldn't send it but I can see Rheinallt looking at me now and saying send it, send it. He knew why I had to leave, in the end, but he never stopped loving me. In order to gain your life, you must lose it, he used to say. It was the guiding principle of his life. You remember that essay he wrote, about you and your white pony and how soon he knew you would be riding away forever. Perhaps that's what you've just done – ridden away – but please darling let it not be forever. I do miss my daughter so much.

Don't worry, darling, I don't propose to act the irate parent and order you back to Oxford. All I ask is that you and Tristan make Isabel and Victoria and the boys welcome at Craig Wen and maintain your father's tradition of keeping an open house.

We'll talk at the end of the week – David and I plan to drive over about Thursday. Take care, cariad, and never forget I love you.

Mam

27

'Of all the stupid things to do!'

'For the ninety-fifth time, I had to do it. Lawrence would have understood. So would Heledd's Dad.'

'What?' The argument between Roger and Richard had been going on ever since the others had arrived home from the second excursion to the quarry, but Heledd had been unable to take in what it was all about.

'His head cloth! There was Justin risking his neck on the end of a rope to rescue it, and what does Richard do? Chuck it back! I give up!'

'Are you all right, Heledd?' asked Victoria, bringing her a mug of tea. 'You've gone awfully pale.'

She managed to nod and smile, but her hands trembled as she took the hot mug from Victoria, and some of the tea spilt on her trousers. She heard Isabel say 'She's crying!' in a shocked whisper.

'Push off, you guys,' said Victoria. 'Go and find an outside job for half an hour.' She dropped on her knees by Heledd's chair and steadied the mug by placing her hands over Heledd's. 'Drink some tea, love. We're all getting on your nerves, aren't we? Had we better move out to the b and b?'

'She's opened the letter,' said Roger, hovering responsibly, looking at the mantlepiece. 'It's the letter.'

'Push off, Roger. No, you stay, Iz. Get Heledd some tissues.'

Six months' unshed tears were pouring down Heledd's cheeks, dripping off her chin onto her hands. Victoria and Isabel knelt by her, mopping her face and helping her drink her tea. The anxious tenderness of their dabbing fingers made her weep even harder.

'If you want us to clear out, Heledd, just say. We'll understand,' said Victoria.

Heledd shook her head agitatedly. At last she managed to gulp, 'No, please, I don't want you to leave.' She took a deep breath and looked helplessly at Victoria and Isabel. How could she say to them, did you know that your father and my mother loved each other all along?

Eiry's words in the quadrangle at Jesus College came back to her. 'Talk about star-crossed lovers!' She found herself whispering the words. As Victoria and Isabel stared at her in alarm she said, 'I didn't know, you see. He never said.'

'Said what? Who never said?'

'My father – my mother – your father –' She stopped, then said flatly, 'I didn't know Mam and your Dad were – in love – before. Before she married Dad.'

'Glory!' said Victoria. 'You must be the only person on the planet who doesn't. The great Oxford love story!'

'But – what about you? What about your Mam – Mum?'

'Well,' said Victoria, shrugging. 'There you go. I don't worry about it any more. It's not so easy for Iz – being born, you know, after they, after Mum and Dad tried to get together again.' She hugged her sister, then said with a laugh. 'It could have been a lot worse. Rhiannon's not bad, as stepmothers go. We quite like her, don't we, Iz?'

Heledd stared from Victoria to Isabel. They've had just as bad a time as I have, she thought, feeling her eyes welling again. They're my sisters. I've been so selfish.

'I don't want you to go,' she said. 'Craig Wen isn't just mine. It's yours as well.'

'It was horrible of me to say you should sell it,' said Victoria. 'I'll never forgive myself. I don't care how cramped we are in Kipling Villas.'

'Please don't cry any more, Helly,' said Isabel anxiously. 'I don't mind you having my bedroom, honest I don't. You can even paint it, if you like. You don't mind me calling you Helly, do you? Nobody calls me Isabel, only Iz, so I thought you wouldn't mind but I won't if you don't want me to!'

What have I said? thought Heledd. What am I going to do? Everything's turning out so different from what I expected. But I've got to stay here. I've got to. Like Mam says in her letter, I've ridden away. I've made my choice. But what about my sisters?

Of course her mother was wrong about one thing. She hadn't ridden away to be with Tristan. It was ridiculous how everyone was jumping to conclusions. No wonder Tristan was so grumpy with her. She had made him look a fool.

'Don't look so worried, Princess,' said Victoria, standing up. 'Aah! My knees! I must do some yoga. Crumbs, it's getting quite dark. We'd better let the boys back in, then think about what we're going to eat. It's all work in a house like this, isn't it? I haven't done any revision at all. I must get down to it.'

Nevertheless, it was *Feet in Chains* that she returned to after supper.

Heledd took down the original Welsh version and tried to read it but found her attention wandering. She wanted to read her mother's letter again. She remembered her father saying, *in many ways I believe she still loves me . . . but I asked too much of her . . . one day you'll understand . . .*

He must have meant that it had been asking too much of Rhiannon to stop loving David, thought Heledd. What she could not understand, though, was how her mother could love David more than Rheinallt. David was a nice man, a kind man on the whole, despite being irritable with Victoria and Isabel all the time, but he wasn't a *great* man. He wasn't a poet and a hero like her father.

Heledd sat by the fire long after the night lights had burned out and the others had gone to bed, thinking about her father and mother and the terrible mistakes she had made about both of them.

'I thought you were still up.' Tristan had emerged from the box bed, jam jar lantern swinging from his hand, and was standing darkly over her. He spoke softly in Welsh, 'You'd better have this money back.'

He was holding something in his free hand. As her eyes adjusted to the faint light she saw two ten pound notes.

'You can't have forgotten,' said Tristan. 'You sent me money, remember? And a note? It was in the post box all this time.'

'I thought you'd used it,' whispered Heledd. 'Eiry said you didn't have any money.'

'Well, I didn't. I don't. But that doesn't mean you have to give me yours. As well as giving me the key.'

'You were homeless,' said Heledd. 'Like that old lady by the M-Martyrs' Memorial.' It sounded odd, saying 'Martyrs' Memorial' in English at the end of a Welsh sentence.

'Old Kathleen,' said Tristan. 'I know her. She sometimes stops at the hostel I worked at last Christmas. She's Irish. Her house was burned down.'

Heledd whispered, 'They thought my Dad was a house burner. They put him in prison. They thought he was planning to burn David's brother's house down. But it wasn't him, it was me.'

There was another movement in the room and a small torch beam flashed on.

'Sorry.' Ben's voice came in a whisper. 'I just needed to pop outside. Sorry to interrupt.'

They waited for him to feel his way through the kitchen.

'Anyway, better have this back,' said Tristan, thrusting the money at her as though he had not heard her last words.

'I didn't mean to burn the house down,' said Heledd wretchedly. 'But I did light a fire. I was angry with Dad because he wanted me to leave him while he was still alive – while he was dying. I couldn't understand him going to that house when they let him out of prison and not coming to me at Aunt Sioned's. I didn't realise, you see –'

The back kitchen door closed quietly and Ben and his torch reappeared. He said, 'Sorry,' again.

'Shush!' said Tristan.

'I didn't realise,' said Heledd. 'He wanted to see Mam again before he died. He always loved her, you see, right from the very beginning. He came to that house to see her and I spoiled it for him. He loved her,' she repeated in English, seeing Ben standing immobile. 'And I spoiled it.'

'Dear Heledd,' said Ben. 'You couldn't spoil anything.'

'That's the bloody media for you,' said Tristan. 'That Griff! Calling her an arsonist! And now she believes it herself!'

'One day,' said Ben, 'you can explain all this to me, if you feel I need to know.' His eyes were fixed on Heledd.

'I need to explain,' whispered Heledd. 'I need to explain to everyone.'

'No, you don't,' said Tristan. 'Anyway, I don't believe it. If this guy's house had burned down it'd have been all over the papers. They'd have loved it. Welsh Nazis strike again.'

'Do you think we should wake up Vix?' murmured Ben to Tristan. 'I don't feel happy – I know you'll think this strange –'

'What do you think I'm going to do to her?' asked Tristan irritably. 'Do you think I'd lay a finger on Rheinallt's daughter? I'm going to bed now, anyway.' He bent and picked up the two ten pound notes from where Heledd had let them fall onto the rug, and handed them to her.

'No,' she said wearily. 'You must keep it. You need it.'

'I'll survive,' said Tristan. 'You've given me enough. You'd better have this back as well.' He delved into his pocket and dropped the Yale key with the horse shoe keyring into her lap.

'No – keep it – you'll need it next week after we've gone.'

'You weren't planning to stay on yourself then?'

What have I said? thought Heledd. Of course I was. She clutched the key. 'But you can stay,' she said. 'I said you could stay.'

'Well,' said Tristan, glancing shiftily at Ben. 'Actually, I was thinking of going back.'

'To Oxford!'

'I'll need to see my tutor. They may not have me.'

So I can stay, thought Heledd. At the end of the week I shall have Craig Wen to myself after all. I can start putting things right . . . and if I own up to Mam, perhaps she'll understand.

She got to her feet and stumbled up the ladder to the loft. The money and the key to Craig Wen fell onto the rug and once more Tristan bent to gather it all up. Watching him, Ben asked, 'How will you manage in Oxford?'

'No idea,' said Tristan. 'I'll live. Time I went back, whatever.'

'Time for Odysseus to set sail once more?' said Ben with a smile.

'Something like that,' said Tristan. He sniffed, and wiped his nose on his sleeve, then reached up to put the key and the ten pound notes on the shelf above the kitchen range. 'Out of the underworld, anyway.'

28

'Well, here it is.'

Lawrence of Arabia's birthplace was a double-fronted grey stone house with a pointed porch and crisp white paint and a young whitebeam tree in the middle of the front lawn.

'It looks empty.'

'And there's the plaque on the bay window – no, two plaques. Not blue like in Oxford, though.'

'Weird, innit,' said Tristan. 'Us standing here. What are we waiting for? Lawrence's nursemaid wheeling him in his push-chair? It's just the same in Swansea. People stand outside 5 Cwmdonkin Drive as though if they stare hard enough the front door will open and the poet himself will come staggering out.'

'What poet?'

'Dylan Thomas, pea brain.'

'Well,' said Richard uncertainly, after they had stared at the house for a while and taken some photographs. 'I'm glad we came.' Suddenly he struck his hand on his forehead. 'Oh no! Of course, what I should have done is left my headcloth on the step as an offering. Oh, why didn't I think of that? And now it's at the bottom of the quarry!'

'Serves you right,' said Justin.

'No,' said Roger. 'The people who live here would just have chucked it into the bin. "What's this bit of rag some fool has left on our doorstep?"'

'I suppose – oh well. There's still quite a good story to tell the other Arabists when we get back to school.' He sounded disappointed, nonetheless.

‘Where is the house your father grew up in?’ Ben asked Heledd as they walked back through the slushy snow to the pretty main square of Tredmadog.

‘It’s just round the corner from here in Dublin Road.’ Heledd led the way to a terrace of stone cottages. ‘The end cottage.’

‘Do your grandparents still live there? Shall we call?’

‘They died when I was in primary school,’ said Heledd. ‘My grandfather was a school teacher.’

‘Mine too!’ said Ben.

‘Where shall we go now?’ interrupted Justin restlessly. ‘We don’t want to go home yet, do we?’

They ended up driving to Cricieth where the temperature seemed at least ten degrees warmer than it had done at Craig Wen that morning. They bought fish and chips and ate them walking along the beach towards the castle, splashing along the edge of the incoming tide.

‘Did you use to come here with your father?’ Isabel asked Heledd as they paused to hunt for shells in a little bank of shingle. ‘You are lucky having the seaside so near.’

Heledd found herself remembering summer visits to Cricieth when she was very young, long before her mother had run away to Oxford. She would toddle along the beach with her father holding one hand and her mother the other, singing nursery rhymes: *Gee ceffyl bach yn cario ni’n dau* . . . gee up, little horse, carrying us two . . . her parents always sang *ni’n tri,* us *three*. They seemed so happy, it seemed impossible that all the time her mother had been in love with somebody else.

‘Mam liked it here,’ she heard herself say. ‘She liked the sea. Before she ran away.’ Isabel’s eyes widened with shock at Heledd's tone. After a moment she said anxiously, 'But you don't hate Rhiannon, do you? You can't! She's nice!'

Heledd shook her head. 'I was just remembering things,' she whispered. 'When I was little. Before she went away. When Dad was still alive.'

'Come on, you two,' called Victoria. 'Crumbs, Iz, what's the matter?'

Isabel's eyes were full of tears. 'I don't want Helly's Dad to be dead,' she wept. 'Why can't he be alive? Why can't my Mum come home? Why can't we all live together in one big house and nobody be dead?'

'Oh, Iz,' said Victoria. 'If only.' She put one arm round Isabel's shoulder and the other round Heledd's. 'Come on,' she said. 'Just says there's a shop near here where they make fantastic ice cream. Let's go and see if it's open. I can always eat ice cream no matter how cold it is.'

On the way home they parked at a viewpoint overlooking Snowdonia, whose peaks were still covered with snow.

'I suppose this is the nearest I'll get to it this week,' said Justin. 'Pity.'

'I don't see why. It's only Wednesday. And it's thawing.'

'It's just as beautiful from here as it is from the top,' said Tristan with a shudder. 'And you can't fall off it neither.'

'Wrong,' said Justin. 'You've got to climb to the top, believe me.'

They sat in the camper van drinking cans of coke. Outside it had begun to rain again, and Snowdon disappeared into the mist.

'Your actual traditional Welsh weather,' said Tristan. 'Bit different from your part of the world, I daresay,' he said to Ben.

'I expect so,' said Ben. 'I haven't seen it lately.'

'Why's that?'

'Oh, my father was on the wrong side, at the wrong moment . . . we could have gone back, after the amnesty, but by that time –' He fell silent.

'I'd love to go to Arabia,' said Richard.

'Ah, but which part?' asked Ben. 'Syria? Lebanon? Saudi Arabia? Israel stroke Palestine? Or one of the easy ones like Jordan, where they welcome tourists and you can ride a camel down the Wadi Rum just like the man himself?'

'All of them,' said Richard, 'Well, perhaps not Iran or Iraq.'

'Iran is Persia, Richard, not Arabia. Your geography!' Ben threw back his empty coke can at Richard, who caught it and threw it back with a laugh.

'Will you ever go back?' Tristan asked Ben.

'Certainly,' said Ben, '*In sha' Allah* – God willing. I will live in a house near the Street Called Straight and you will all visit me.'

'We'd better be moving,' said Roger. 'The van's getting steamed up with your hot air. Your turn to drive, Rich, but watch the road, it's still pretty slushy.'

Richard rolled his eyes at the others as he changed places with his twin. They drove along the foot of the towering mountains with the rain behind them, then turned north for Bethesda. As they drove along the main street of the old quarry town Victoria asked Heledd, 'Is there a swimming pool here? I just thought, we could come down for a swim later and have a shower at the same time.'

'Yes – there it is, just up there.'

'Have you lot brought swimming kit?' asked Roger. 'I haven't.'

'Drat, no. Never mind, we've got towels, we can still use the showers. You too, Tristan. We've been polite about you for too long.'

Tristan groaned. Heledd thought, I'll get out some more of Dad's clothes for him.

'Thank goodness, the rain's stopping,' said Richard as they crawled up the hill to the village and turned into the lane to Craig Wen. 'Oops! It's still quite snowy here. Slowly does it. It looks as though a tractor's been up here, Heledd. Would that be your neighbour?'

They breasted the last rise and looked across the snowy moor at Craig Wen under its rock.

Parked outside the house was Griff Jenkins's smart new Land Rover. Next to it was another car, a small red car. Aunt Sioned's car.

29

'Disgusting,' said Sioned Jones, Rheinallt's elder sister. She sniffed into the ripe cavern of the box bed. 'Filthy! On drugs as well, no doubt! And where have they all been sleeping? That's what I'd like to know!'

Griff Jenkins was beginning to feel ashamed of himself for letting Sioned involve him in this expedition. 'I can't smell any dope,' he said feebly. 'And it's no worse than the camping field on the last night of the Eisteddfod. They've washed up, and the fire's banked up as well.'

'Hippies!' said Sioned. 'If that woman is going to let Heledd grow up into a hippy I'm going to have something to say about it!' She marched into the parlour, still exclaiming about the smell. Griff looked round uneasily. He took in the books scattered on the rag rug, and the key on the horse-shoe keyring on the mantlepiece. He looked in the boiler and let the hot lid drop with a clatter. He poked the fire and put on a fresh log.

'Well, it's not in here,' Sioned reported. 'Mind you, she used to sleep in the *croglofft*. Hold the ladder a minute while I look.' She climbed up and peered into the loft. 'Well, at least it looks as though the girls have been sleeping up here. Dear, dear, did you ever see such a mess? Here we are, here's her Dad's old case.' She pulled it across the floorboards by the handle and handed it down to Griff. The lid was not fastened; it flapped open before Griff could catch it safely, and a cluster of envelopes and paperback books slithered to the floor.

'I don't like doing this,' he said as Sioned climbed down again and dived at the envelopes on the floor. 'We should have waited and asked her. It was her he sent the poem to.'

'She's still a minor,' said Sioned. 'She's got no rights in the matter. I'm a trustee, I am, just as much as her mother. That woman shouldn't encourage her. If I'd known we were going to have all this trouble I'd have kept her in Maeshafren with me –' She was looking through the envelopes as she spoke, her fingers snatching angrily at the contents of each one. 'What's this? This is Rheinallt's handwriting – no, it's another of his letters. He was always writing to her, goodness knows what about.' She looked up as Griff made an embarrassed noise. 'Well, all right, I won't look if you're so particular. In my day a girl wouldn't have been allowed to keep her letters secret, even letters from her father. But she ought to take better care of them. They'll want to publish his letters one day. Now then, here it is.'

She unfolded the creased A4 sheets on which the poem was written, and scanned the first page. 'Feet of what?' After a few seconds she handed it to Griff. 'I can't make head nor tail of it. Mind, he was a bit off his head at the end, if you ask me. See that dedication to Rhiannon? That proves his mind was wandering. You see what you think. I'm going to get all those stinking blankets outside and burn them.'

'It's raining,' said Griff. He held the sheets of paper delicately. He knew he should not read the poem, and he knew that nothing on earth would stop him. He sat down, ignoring Sioned's horrified cries as she pulled quilts and blankets out of the box bed.

'Put them back.'

Neither of them had noticed the camper van driving up, nor Heledd getting out. She stood in the doorway, her fair hair standing out in a halo round her head and her chin held high.

'So there you are, Miss!' exclaimed Sioned, tossing aside a blanket and advancing across the kitchen, hands on hips. 'And just what's been going on, if you please?'

'Put those blankets back,' said Heledd, shutting the door behind her.

'What, these stinking, disgusting rags?'

'They don't belong to you,' said Heledd. 'This is my house, and those are my blankets. And that,' she turned on Griff, 'is my poem.'

'Yes,' said Griff. 'Yes. I'm sorry.' He handed her the pages. 'But Heledd – '

'Your poem!' said Sioned. 'Your blankets! Don't you speak to me like that! You're not eighteen yet and until you are you've got to do as we say. And we don't say that stinking hippies can stay here taking drugs and turning Rheinallt's house into a slum! Look at this! Stinking!' She pulled another blanket out of the box bed.

'We haven't been taking drugs,' said Heledd. 'My friends aren't hippies. We aren't doing anything wrong. Now will you please go away.'

'Well!' cried Sioned. 'I've never been spoken to like that in my life. If these are the manners you've picked up in Oxford I don't think much of them. Ordering me out of my own brother's house!'

'You were burgling it,' said Heledd.

'We ought to go, Mrs Jones,' said Griff. 'I said we shouldn't have –'

'You give him back that poem,' said Sioned. 'It's an important document. It ought to be in safe hands. It ought to be published.'

'Well,' said Griff. 'I'm not sure. It's quite a strange poem. It might be better to leave it for a while.' He flinched at Heledd's contemptuous look.

Outside, in the camper van, the others looked worriedly out of the steamy windows at the two strange vehicles.

'That Land Rover belongs to that guy that was here before,' said Tristan. 'Griff Thingy. He's after the poem.'

'Do you think we should go in?' said Victoria. 'You go and have a reccy, Tristan, you can speak Welsh, and you know the guy as well.'

'Not to mention being the cleanest and most respectable looking of us,' said Richard. Tristan blew a raspberry at him as he ducked past Ben out of the van, then ran through the rain to the cottage door. As he opened it he heard Griff Jenkins say, 'I'm not sure what it's going to do for his reputation.'

'What do you mean?' Tristan saw a small angry firecracker of a woman with wild, greying hair, whom he realised from her resemblance to Heledd must be Rheinallt's elder sister. She recoiled in horror at the sight of Tristan.

'What do you mean by that?' he asked. 'It's a bloody good poem.'

'And who do you think you are?' snapped Sioned.

'He's a friend of mine,' said Heledd. 'He's been staying here with me and the others.'

'It's different from anything else he ever wrote,' said

Griff. 'I'm not saying – but people won't know what to make of it. Not yet, anyway. Better if you hang on to it for now, Heledd.'

'I intend to,' said Heledd.

'You intend to!' repeated Sioned. 'You intend to! Hoity toity! Aren't we the snooty little Oxford girl all of a sudden!' She snatched the manuscript of the poem from Heledd's hand. 'Can't you hear what Mr Jenkins is saying? The poem's no good! He's from the Arts Council! He should know! Your Dad wrote it when he was dying! You didn't see the state of him in the end!'

'No,' said Heledd. 'You wouldn't let me.'

'His mind was going!' said Sioned. 'Is that how you want him to be remembered?'

'Give it back to me, please.'

'Never!' said Sioned. 'The trouble that man caused, ever. I'm sick to death of it.' She tore the manuscript in half, crumpled the pieces into a ball and threw it at the fire. It hit the edge of the grate and bounced back onto the rug. Heledd snatched it up and gave it to Tristan who stuffed it into his pocket.

'You'd give it to that dirty hippy!' cried Sioned.

'I know it's safe with him,' said Heledd.

'Are you sure?' said Griff. 'He gave me the impression he didn't have any time for Rheinallt.'

'Wrong,' said Tristan. 'I've got a lot of time for Rheinallt.'

'And what would you know about it?' asked Sioned scornfully.

'He knows,' said Heledd. 'He's clever. He's at Oxford University. He's studying Latin and Greek, like Dad.'

'It's a good poem,' said Tristan to Sioned. 'Trust me.'

'Hoity toity!' said Sioned again. Suddenly, all her fierceness seemed to collapse. She sat down at the table and blew her nose. 'I don't know,' she said. 'I can't make head or tail of any of it. In my day people wrote poems about the mountains and the forests, not about sand and feet. And they kept themselves clean and they didn't take drugs either.'

'*Aros mae'r mynyddau mawr*,' quoted Griff. 'Still the mighty mountains stand.'

'That's it,' said Sioned. 'I suppose you young people don't think anything of a good old-fashioned poem like that. I won a prize for recitation at the Urdd Eisteddfod with that poem when I was in the primary school.'

'Good old Ceiriog,' said Tristan cheerfully, gathering up the pile of blankets from where Sioned had dropped them and tossing them back into the box bed. 'My party piece was the cuckoo one – *O diolch iti, gwcw* –' he recited, falsetto. 'I tell you, Swansea had never heard the like.'

Sioned began to look rather daunted. She blew her nose again and pulled a packet of cigarettes out of her pocket. She lit one, then offered the packet to Griff, who shook his head. After a moment she held the packet grudgingly out in Tristan's direction.

'Thanks,' said Tristan. 'But no thanks.' He took his asthma inhaler out of his coat pocket and sucked on it.

'Aunt Sioned, all the others are still outside, and it's raining,' said Heledd. 'I must call them to come in.'

Sioned said, 'Go on then, I don't want anyone catching pneumonia on my account. Where are you from then?' she asked Tristan. 'You aren't from round here.'

'No,' agreed Tristan. Then he relented. 'My Nain and

Taid came from Bethesda. My Taid's buried in the cemetery there.'

'He is, is he? What was his name, then?'

Trying to work out which branch of the Vaughans Tristan might be connected to seemed to placate Aunt Sioned somewhat, but she frosted over again when the others were introduced, despite the fulsome politeness of the Clare twins. 'It's such an honour to be staying here,' said Richard, shaking her hand. She's shy of English people with posh accents, thought Heledd, watching her snatch her hand away. And she still thinks we might be taking drugs and having sex. However, she accepted a cup of tea made by Tristan and ate a chocolate biscuit. Griff stood by the kitchen range talking to Justin about climbing. Why didn't he just go? Did he still want to get hold of the poem?

At last Aunt Sioned announced that she couldn't sit round here chatting all night, it was a two-hour drive back to Maeshafren. Looking disappointed, Griff said that he too must be going. Heledd followed them outside to their vehicles, leaving the Oxford party rolling their eyes at each other in relief. Darkness had fallen but it had stopped raining.

'Well,' said Sioned, getting into her red Metro and winding down the window. 'I hope your mother knows what she's doing, that's all I can say. But she should have told me. I'm a trustee as well.' When Heledd did not reply she went on, 'You should have a bit of sense, Heledd, and think about Mr Jenkins's proposition. Nobody has more respect for your father than he has.'

Heledd began to shake her head, but her aunt exclaimed, 'Well, what else can we do with this place?

We'll never sell it to anybody else! Who'd want to live here with no toilets or 'lectric? Look at it! It's all very well camping out for a week –'

Griff Jenkins turned back from his Land Rover and came and stood by Heledd. 'Perhaps you're planning to keep it for a holiday cottage,' he suggested. 'Mind you, I don't know what your father would have thought of that idea. The home of Wales's greatest modern poet a holiday home for a family of Oxford academics?' There was an apologetic note in his voice, as though forcing himself to speak despite his better judgement. 'I don't mean to be nasty, like, but I'd burn it down first, if it were mine.' He looked from Heledd to Sioned and backed down. 'Sorry, I didn't mean that.'

You did mean that, you hypocrite, thought Heledd. You're trying to wind me up. Aunt Sioned told you I was an arsonist and you're quite disappointed because I'm not. She stared at him with loathing and he said, 'Sorry,' again before climbing into his Land Rover and starting up the engine. Its wheels churned up the muddy slush as he turned round and drove away.

'He didn't mean it,' said Sioned. 'Now then, you tell your Mam I'll be ringing her up. We've got to have a proper talk about all this. I don't think we should turn the Arts Council down without thinking about it seriously. Dear me, I'd feel happier if you were coming back to Maeshafren with me but if your Mam and that man she's got her leg over are coming tomorrow I'd better leave well alone. But I don't like it, and I shall tell her so.'

Heledd cried, 'Why do you have to talk like that? As if they're doing something dirty! David is Mam's husband!'

'Hm!' Sioned turned the ignition key of the car several times before the engine fired. 'Your father was her husband! I didn't expect you to forget that, Heledd, you of all people!' She drove off jerkily. skidding a little at the top of the lane, then remembering to switch on the car headlights. Heledd walked to the gate and pushed it shut, watching until the two pairs of rear lights had disappeared over the hill.

Turning, she looked back at her home. Moonlight fell across the old roof, and a last patch of snow slid from the slates to the ground. Smoke rose from the chimney, and candlelight shone from the small windows.

In order to gain your life, you must lose it, her father had written in his last letter, and for a while she had believed that what he meant was that she should destroy Craig Wen, the place where they had been so happy, to keep it safe from being corrupted and spoiled by people who did not understand it.

Well, she thought, if anyone like Griff Jenkins ever gets hold of it I will. He'd spoil it quicker than anyone. But that was not what her father wanted. She understood quite clearly now. Her father wanted her to open the doors, not close them.

A yellow oblong of light appeared as Victoria opened the cottage door and shouted, 'Heledd! Have they gone?'

That's what caused all the trouble before, she thought, returning Victoria's wave. When the original Heledd in the poem closed the doors and turned away the visitor at the gate. Not that Isabel and Victoria and the others were likely to declare war if she turned them away, but they'd certainly never be friends again, and that would be terrible.

After supper Tristan took the torn and crumpled sheets of the poem from his pocket and flattened them out carefully on the kitchen table.

'You ought to copy it out,' he told Heledd. 'Then you can keep the original safe. You'll have to get it repaired.'

'I've got an A4 pad if you want to do it now, Heledd,' said Victoria, peering over Heledd's shoulder. 'Is that your Dad's handwriting? What's that bit at the top about Rhiannon?

'The poem's dedicated to her,' said Heledd. 'So I must do a copy for her too. I'll give it to her tomorrow.'

30

'Oh dear,' said Rhiannon, in the kitchen at Craig Wen late the following morning, listening to her stepdaughters describing yesterday's events. 'It's my fault. I should have let Sioned know you were all staying here instead of letting her find out from the Davieses Tanygraig. All I wanted to do was to give you all a bit of peace for a few days, but she'll have seen it as me acting behind her back.' She turned to David. 'We'll have to go back via Maeshafren and see her.'

'She was mad at first,' said Victoria. 'She was going on about us taking drugs. Tristan reckoned that Griff chap had been winding her up. But she stayed for tea. She said to Tristan, why don't you make us a cup of tea, if you're not too proud to fill a kettle with your Latin and your Greek! She took quite a liking to him in the end. More than the rest of us.'

'Where is that young man?' asked David. 'He's got some explaining to do.'

'You're not to shout at him!' said Isabel. 'It's so sad! His grandma died. He calls her his Nain. That's Welsh for grandma.'

'You all thought he'd eloped with Heledd,' said Victoria. 'Don't think we don't realise.'

'I knew he couldn't have done, really,' said Rhiannon.

'He should have told us about his grandmother,' said David. 'We could have got him some help.'

'He doesn't like talking about his grandma,' said Isabel. 'He doesn't think it's anybody else's business.'

'Yes, well,' said David, 'I still need to talk to him, if he wants to go back to Oxford. His tutor's mad keen to have him, but what's he going to do for money? There's a small matter of the fees.' He glanced at Rhiannon, who was frowning slightly. 'Sorry,' he said. 'It'll do later. What about a cup of tea or coffee for us, you girls, if you're not too proud to fill a kettle for your old Dad?'

Heledd listened to her stepsisters chatting to their father, conscious of her mother's quiet scrutiny. She made herself smile but could think of nothing to say. She yearned to be alone with her mother, and dreaded it at the same time.

'I don't know what you're planning for lunch,' said Rhiannon, 'but we've bought some pizzas. Can we heat them up in the oven?'

'You wouldn't believe the cooking we've been doing on that old range,' said Victoria. 'It makes the best baked potatoes ever! And as for Heledd's pancakes, they're fantastic.'

'Well, you seem to have made yourselves comfortable, in a chaotic sort of way,' said David, looking round the warm, untidy kitchen. 'Despite no video or CD players.'

'No adults, that's been the main thing,' said Victoria, baring her teeth at her father.

'Don't mind me,' said David. 'I'm only the banker. You all look a lot cleaner than I expected,' he added as the boys came trooping back into the kitchen laden with logs and buckets of water. 'Even him.' He nodded brusquely at Tristan, who had allowed Heledd to give him some of her father's old clothes and was hardly recognisable.

'Sports Centre,' said Victoria. 'We went this morning. It was the best shower I've ever had, even though the hot water kept going off.'

'We had a bath in front of the fire one day,' Isabel began to tell Rhiannon. 'It was lovely. We heated up the water in the boiler and shared. It was all steamy like a sauna. It's all right,' she said as her father raised his eyebrows. 'The boys went out. They didn't look.'

'I should think not,' said David. 'Now then, what about those pizzas? I'm starving. And this afternoon you lot can take me for a walk on the hills. I'd love to see these standing stones Rheinallt used to talk about. I bet you know them, don't you, Heledd?'

Heledd nodded, blushing. Her father had shown her every standing stone, every Bronze Age barrow, every Iron Age fort on the wild uplands which stretched from Craig Wen to the Carneddau. I mustn't lose that, she thought. I mustn't forget.

He had shown her mother, too, and she had not forgotten. Perhaps she remembered walking along the beach at Cricieth as well. Perhaps she had not put it all ruthlessly behind her when she left to live with David. *There's so much of my life I need to share with you,* she had written.

It was cold on the high moorland. They scrambled across the rocky ground, slipping on bits of frost-encrusted moss and grass and pockets of snow. The experienced walkers, Justin, Roger and Richard, made the fastest progress, competitively pursued by Ben and Victoria. David followed more slowly with Tristan who had had to be coerced into his boots. David was talking hard, and Heledd could see Tristan looking stubbornly into the distance. Isabel hung back with Heledd and Rhiannon, holding on to Rhiannon's hand. 'We might see the wild ponies,' she informed her. 'They came down for their hay this morning but they went off before you got here, so you missed them, but I'm sure they went off this way.'

'Has Heledd taken you to see her old pony at Tanygraig Farm yet?'

'Oh yes, we went this morning. It's a lovely farm, but there weren't any lambs yet. Shani was very pleased to see Helly, she neighed at her like anything. She's too old to be ridden any more, but you'll never guess, she's allowed into the kitchen! I do wish we had a pony,' said Isabel, tugging earnestly at Rhiannon's hand. 'Even an old one that we couldn't ride. Or a donkey. Helly would help me look after it, you wouldn't have to do a thing.'

'Well,' said Rhiannon. 'We'll have to see.' She was looking at Heledd. 'How were the Davieses?' she asked.

'They were fine,' said Heledd, embarrassed. 'They said they hoped you'd call.' But they had been offended, she could tell, because she had decided to stay with her English friends at Craig Wen instead of returning to the comfortable little bed they had made up for her in the farmhouse. Iwan had been quite nasty about it. 'You're all for the *Sais* now, I see,' he'd said. 'You don't want to know your old neighbours any more, with your new fine friends.' But there had been a look of envy on his face as he spoke. It must be a lonely life on the farm. He probably saw very few people of his own age now that he had left school, apart from at chapel and the Aelwyd. There was no pub in the village. I should have asked him over, thought Heledd. I didn't think.

'Then yesterday we went out in the camper van,' continued Isabel. 'Where did we go yesterday, Helly?'

'We went to Tremadog, and Cricieth,' said Heledd, avoiding her mother's eye.

'It was nice at the seaside,' said Isabel. 'We had fish and chips and ice cream. We're having a lovely time. We haven't got to go home yet, have we?'

'Well,' said Rhiannon. 'Not until Saturday, perhaps. Your mother's been telephoning. I think she'd like to come over on Sunday.'

'I don't want to see her,' said Isabel. 'I hate her. She ran off and left us and I don't want to see her.'

That's what I used to say to myself about Mam, thought Heledd as she listened to her mother remonstrating kindly with Isabel. I was so angry with her.

'We're so hopeless, we grown-ups,' Rhiannon was saying. 'We do silly, selfish things and make all sorts of bad decisions, and then we try to put things right and we get into even worse messes.'

'You're not like that,' said Isabel, stamping on a frozen tuft of grass.

'I'm afraid I am,' said Rhiannon.

'Iz! Iz!' Victoria and Ben had appeared over the top of the ridge and were waving wildly. 'The ponies! Come and see!'

As Isabel scrambled ahead of them up the steep path Rhiannon said to Heledd, 'You all seem to have been happy here this week.' Heledd nodded shyly, 'I'm sorry we all got the wrong end of the stick about Tristan.'

'I forgot he might be here,' said Heledd, watching where she was placing her feet. 'He was sleeping on that tower because he had nowhere else to go so I gave him the key to Craig Wen, but then I forgot.'

'Your father would have done the same,' said Rhiannon. 'I'm glad it's worked out the way it has. It's good for Craig Wen to be lived in again.' She hesitated, then continued, 'I know how much you missed Craig Wen and wanted to come home, but I'm not sure what your long-term plans are. If you really can't bear Oxford, we can't do anything until you're sixteen, but after that, if you really wanted to come back – do your A Levels in Bangor perhaps – well, we'll see if it can be arranged. I'll fix things with Sioned. If it's really what you want.'

They had reached the top of the ridge where Isabel was impatiently waiting. The wind whipped their faces as they gazed at the snow-covered peaks which surrounded them.

'Look!' said Isabel. 'Rhiannon, look, the ponies!'

I can stay, thought Heledd. I can stay here forever. She staggered a little as the wind, and the knowledge, hit her.

I can stay at Craig Wen, she thought, repeating the words carefully to herself to get used to them.

'Please say we can have a pony in Oxford, Rhiannon,' Isabel was saying. 'Oh please, please say we can. Helly will help me look after it and I won't have any more riding lessons so that would save money. Helly could teach me, Mrs Davies says she's a very good rider. You will help me, Helly, won't you?'

'For a fourteen-year-old,' said Rhiannon, 'you've got some terribly old-fashioned ambitions, darling.'

'But I won't be a horsy bore like Dad says, I promise.'

'Well,' said Rhiannon. 'It's really up to Heledd. What if she prefers Wales to Oxford?'

The light in Isabel's face went out. 'Well,' she said after a moment, 'I wouldn't blame her.'

Heledd looked at her stepsister's downcast face. The ground seem to shift under her feet. She thought, Dad would never, ever forgive me if I turned my back on Isabel now.

31

In the quadrangle of Jesus College the daffodils were in bloom and the late afternoon sun was shining for St. David's Day. Eiry, a daffodil pinned to the faded black cotton of her short commoner's gown, herded Heledd and her friends out of the sharp March wind into the dining hall, to wait while the college guests finished their tea.

Richard let out a cry of joy at the sight of the Lawrence portrait. 'There's nothing for it,' he said. 'I shall have to come to Jesus. Imagine having one's breakfast every morning watched over by Lawrence of Arabia!'

'He doesn't look a bit like Peter O'Toole,' said Victoria.

'Well, he wouldn't,' said Roger. 'Lawrence was only five-feet-five tall, to start with.'

'There's a fad, at the moment, for the haircut,' said Eiry. 'Like on that sculpture of him in the chapel. Very like yours, in fact.'

'Well, I never!'

The door to the dining hall opened, and Tristan came in under the carved dragons. A washed, fed and shaved Tristan in a moderately respectable jacket with a short black gown, slightly different in cut from Eiry's, slipping backwards off his shoulders.

'Your tutor's been looking for you,' said Eiry.

'I know,' said Tristan. 'I'm lying low. I'm brassed off with this prodigal son bit.'

'Best Classics scholar since Rheinallt,' said Eiry in a mocking sing-song.

'De-da, de-da! *Iesu!* I mean, it's not even true. Your father,' he said to Heledd, 'has got a lot to answer for.'

'Are you still living on St. Mary's tower?' asked Richard.

'Just for now,' said Tristan. 'I do like a bit of fresh air.'

'Aren't you nervous?' asked Eiry. 'I mean, the Principal, and all.'

'No,' said Tristan. 'Are you nervous, Princess?'

Heledd shook her head.

'Come on, then. Your Mam's here. I'll hide behind you lot,' he added to the others.

'Gosh!' said Eiry as they left the dining hall and looked across the quadrangle at the entrance to the college chapel. 'There's a bigger crowd than there was last year. Look, Heledd, there's the Professor of Celtic, she's the first woman to have the job ever.'

Heledd frowned, unable to distinguish which of the milling figures in billowing black robes Eiry was pointing at. One of the figures turned, and Heledd saw her mother waving at her, looking oddly unfamiliar, but magnificent, in her cap and gown over her flowing lavender silk skirt. She heard Roger catch his breath and remembered him saying, ages ago, in the Eagle and Child, 'Your mother is so beautiful.'

He saw her looking at him, and a faint blush coloured his fair cheeks. 'I don't know what it is about your mother,' he said.

'Oh glory,' said Victoria. 'No wonder the rest of us girls don't get a look in. Even you,' she said to Justin. 'You weren't going to come until you heard Rhiannon was going to be there.'

'Yes, I was,' said Justin.

'Hello,' said Rhiannon, smiling at them all. 'There you are, Heledd, I want you to come and meet the Principal. Eiry, I can leave you to look after the others, can't I?'

'So this is Rheinallt's daughter,' said the Principal, shaking her hand. 'I hear you're honouring us this afternoon, my dear. And the young Vaughan, I see. I'm very sorry to hear about your grandmother, Tristan.'

Tristan nodded grudgingly. Don't be rude, Heledd begged him silently. Don't spoil it.

'I think we're needed in the chapel,' said the Principal urbanely. 'I hope I'm sitting next to you, Rhiannon.'

'Unfortunately I'm playing the organ, Principal, otherwise it would have been delightful.'

'Oh gawd,' said Tristan as he and Heledd followed Rhiannon and the Principal into the chapel. 'Delaightful! So sorry to hear about your grandmother, Tristan! As if he'd ever understand the first thing about my grandmother!' Rhiannon looked back over her shoulder with raised eyebrows. 'Biting the hand that feeds us, are we?' she asked.

'It hasn't fed me yet,' said Tristan, 'that you'd notice.'

'You must have faith,' said Rhiannon. 'The gods are on your side.'

Tristan scowled, then cheered up as they passed the stone bust of T. E. Lawrence in the entrance to the chapel. 'Richard must think he's died and gone to heaven,' he said to Heledd. As they moved slowly through the crowd, he asked, 'You got the poem?'

Heledd nodded. She was holding a smart new folder with a photograph of her father on the cover. It contained two copies of *Traed Tywod*, written in her best handwriting on sheets of pearly cream hand-made paper which her mother had sent for from a special shop in London. She was trying not to clutch the folder in case she left sweaty fingerprints on her father's face. She opened it to give Tristan his copy of the poem but he said, 'Keep it until we need it. I may drop it.'

An undergraduate Heledd recognised as one of Eiry's flatmates ushered them to seats at the altar end of the choir near the lectern. She rested the folder on her knee, looking at her father on the cover. What do you think of this, Dad? she asked him silently. Are you glad I'm here? Am I doing what you wanted me to do? She glanced sideways at Tristan and wondered if he were thinking of his grandmother and asking her the same questions.

The service began. A Welsh hymn was sung, someone read from the Bible in very clumsy Welsh. Heledd wondered why there were no daffodils on the altar, although virtually every member of the congregation was wearing one, then remembered that it was Lent. She listened to her mother playing the organ and remembered David telling her about how often her father used to play it when he was a student.

I wish I could play the organ like Dad, she thought, then immediately remembered the time she had said this to him, when he was still alive, and he had replied, 'I wish I could paint like you, Heledd.'

A nearby candle cast a flickering light over the photograph of her father. It was almost as though he were smiling at her in that shy, twinkling way he had, a smile she had almost forgotten because for so many months she had believed that he must be angry and disappointed with her. Oh Dad, she thought. You have forgiven me, haven't you?

'And now,' the Principal was saying, in English, 'for something rather special, to commemorate a dearly loved old student who died so tragically young last year, but who lives on through his poetry.'

Tristan nudged her. 'This is us,' he said.

Heledd stood at the lectern, Tristan by her side. She cleared her throat. 'Before he died,' she began, 'my father, Rheinallt, wrote a poem.' She repeated the words in English. The congregation went very quiet.

'He dedicated it,' she said, 'to my mother.'

‘I can’t believe it! I can’t believe it!’ Eiry was sniffing and wiping her eyes with tissues. ‘What a sensation! His last poem! *I loved you, so I drew these tides of men into my hands* – oh my God! Everybody was in tears!’

‘Yeah, even the ones who didn’t understand a word,’ said Tristan.

‘That first bit wasn’t by Dad,’ Heledd explained anxiously to Eiry. ‘He put it at the beginning because he used to quote it at Mam.’

‘Rhiannon was in floods,’ said Justin. ‘Doctor Dave was having to hold her up.’

‘He wasn’t the only one,’ said Roger, looking at his brother.

‘I’m glad you explained things in English a bit,’ said Victoria to Heledd as they waited for their parents in the dusk outside the chapel. ‘But I didn’t understand the middle bit, vanitatus something.’

‘*Vanitas vanitatum, et omnia vanitas*,’ said Tristan. “Vanity of vanities, saith the preacher, all is vanity.” Ecclesiastes.’

‘You mean he’s saying he only did all that climbing up television masts and stuff out of vanity? To show off to Rhiannon? And not because he believed in it?’

‘That’s what he was asking himself, all the time,’ said Tristan. ‘So he’s warning us all not to make a fake hero out of him, like people did with Lawrence of Arabia. Griff Jenkins will be as sick as hell when he reads it.’

‘That’s why,’ murmured Richard. He breathed in shakily. ‘That’s why Lawrence is important, isn’t it? Because he knew all that, didn’t he? Just like Rheinallt.’ He took out a handkerchief and blew his nose fiercely.

Heledd thought of the Arab headdress at the bottom of the quarry.

'But it didn't stop him,' said Tristan. 'The poem's about that too.'

'But he risked everything!'

'That's what poets are for,' said Tristan.

'Heledd! Darling!' Rhiannon appeared out of the subdued crowd and hugged her daughter. 'I'm so proud of you! Rheinallt would have been so proud of you! Oh look at me, I can't turn the tap off!' She pulled a handkerchief from the sleeve of her gown and wiped her eyes. 'You were wonderful too, Tristan,' she said, kissing him on the cheek.

'Great Scott,' said David, coming up and putting his arm around his wife's waist. 'I need a drink. I'm exhausted with all this emotion. Come on, you lot, dinner.'

'It's like being a student already,' said Victoria to Heledd as they joined a crowd of undergraduates making for the dining hall. 'However did Rhiannon fix for us all to stay to dinner?'

The noise in the dining hall was terrific. Isabel held tight to Heledd's hand and sat between her and Eiry who was shouting introductions up and down the table. David and Rhiannon were sitting at High Table with the Principal and the Professor of Celtic and other senior academics.

'It's a bit different from Craig Wen, isn't it?' said Ben into Heledd's right ear. She smiled and nodded.

'Do you wish you were still there?'

Heledd thought for a moment.

Ben said, 'We were very happy, weren't we?'

She nodded slowly. 'I wanted to be there on my own,'

she said. 'But it was better, in the end, with us all together.'

'I wish I was still there,' said Victoria, leaning across the table to listen to them. 'It was the best time. It seemed awful leaving Craig Wen all empty and dark. I bet it misses us like anything.'

No fire, no candle, thought Heledd.

'Don't be sad, Heledd,' said Ben. He touched the back of her hand with one of his fingers, then removed it quickly. She shook her head.

'What's the matter?'

She whispered, 'There wasn't enough time,' remembering the Davieses hurt faces.

'But it'll be Easter soon. And summer's coming!'

'Meanwhile, it's back to the coal face with a vengeance,' said Victoria, grimacing at Eiry. 'A Levels,' she explained.

'Oh, poor you.'

'At least I can swot in peace,' continued Victoria. 'We've swopped bedrooms. Iz shares with Heledd now.'

This had been Heledd's suggestion, ecstatically received by both Victoria and Isabel. Heledd was finding it curiously comforting to share a room with Isabel and her model ponies. It was like being thirteen again herself, and not having to think about things and make decisions, except about easy things, like making sure she didn't forget Iwan Davies Tanygraig and the rest of her Bangor friends next time she went home to Craig Wen.

She looked down the table at Tristan who was staring over her head at the Lawrence portrait. His jaw worked absently on a mouthful of roast lamb. He looked weary, as though the noise and clatter in the dining hall were getting him down and he longed for the peace of St. Mary's tower.

Not that he really was living there, of course. He was back in his room in the Ship Street Annexe, whatever that meant. Heledd had overheard David talking to her mother about it. It seemed that the college had put Tristan in the way of some financial help towards his fees. And there had been talk of student loans.

'But however you look at it,' David had said, 'he's going to end up ten thousand quid in the red by the time he graduates. If he makes it. Even if he doesn't.'

Ten thousand pounds.

Was Craig Wen worth more than ten thousand pounds?

She picked up her glass of water and gulped some down, trying to put the terrible question out of her mind. 'No,' she whispered. 'No.' No one seemed to be listening. On her left Isabel was giggling at a teasing remark of Richard's. On her right she could hear Ben telling the bearded student on his far side about the political situation in Syria. 'We may be able to return to Damascus soon,' he was saying. He turned to Heledd. 'One day, I hope, I will be able to show you my city.'

Did he mean just her, or all of them? wondered Heledd. She'd heard that young men and women weren't allowed to mix in Arab countries. Had he forgotten this? Somehow she didn't think so.

But I could travel, she thought. Like Dad going by bus to Greece and Turkey when he was seventeen with fifty pounds in his pocket. Like Lawrence of Arabia walking across the desert looking for Crusader castles. I could go to the Holy Land too. Jerusalem and Jericho and the Sea of Galilee.

I should like that, she thought, but only if I can always come home to Craig Wen.

Even as the thought formed in her mind, she knew she was asking too much. She had no right to expect to cling to the past and embrace the future as well. She had to lose her life in order to gain it. She had to make a choice. As her father had done.

She turned her head to meet Ben's serious gaze. 'It may have changed,' she said. 'It may not be like you remember.'

'Yes,' said Ben. 'So it may.'

He's not afraid, thought Heledd. He's not afraid, so I mustn't be either. She caught her breath, in awe of the sudden new largeness of the world. For an instant was she back on St. Mary's Tower looking out over the city. *Holl deyrnasoedd y byd* . . . all the kingdoms of the world . . . and yet now it did not seem that she was being tempted to sell her soul to the devil.

'So,' said Ben. 'Heledd?'

'Yes,' she said. 'Yes.

Other titles in the
PONT YOUNG ADULT *series*

The novel in which Heledd of *No Fire, No Candle* first appears

Something's Burning

Mary Oldham

Something's burning in the hearts of four young people in a Welsh border town.

Barbara Dawes burns to be Welsh, to be thin, to have a boyfriend. She's in love with Lord Byron the poet and, more painfully, with Byron Tudor in her class at school.

And Byron Tudor wouldn't mind being adored by her either, if only she weren't what he calls a 'White Settler' from England. He burns to do something for Wales, though what exactly he doesn't know.

Hywel Tudor is Byron's elder brother, a farmer and horse-breeder. Barbara may think he's too old and pushy, but even he is someone whose feelings can be hurt.

Who knows what fire is eating up the heart of Heledd Aeronwy Jones, the mysterious new girl from North Wales who refuses to speak to anyone? Why did she scratch 'I am a political prisoner' on a toilet wall? Who has imprisoned her? Heledd's dumb and desperate anger draws each one of them, like moths to a flame.

ISBN 1 85902 119 0

£4.95

Alwena's Garden

Mary Oldham

Alwena Morgan lives at Plas Idaleg, a ruined mansion lost in the remote Welsh hills. Here she struggles to recover from a long illness which has left her with painfully arthritic arms and legs and a growing fear of the outside world. Self-conscious of her twisted limbs, she does not want to go back to school or have to face people of her own age.

Which is how her over-protective father, Roscoe Morgan, likes it. He wants to keep her safe, keep her and Plas Idaleg to himself. So when a group of sixth formers arrive to study the Plas for their A level History project, Alwena's father is touchy and suspicious, especially of Gareth Lloyd, who dreams of being an architect and falls in love with the house and its surroundings. For Alwena, Gareth's arrival certainly creates problems but also leads to discoveries that will change her life.

'Strong in plot, characterisation, dialogue and setting, this novel will prove popular with 13-year-olds and indeed older teenagers.'—*The School Librarian*

ISBN 1 85902 438 6

£5.95

Winner of the Tir na n-Og prize

Shampoo & Seawater

Nicola Davies

Funny, isn't it, how a single flash of light can change your whole life?

Rhian has her future all planned, with a full-time hairdressing job waiting for her when she leaves school.

But after she loses consciousness on the mountainside, those plans go haywire. Nothing is ever the same again.

Was it that one bright light that started it? This invasion of her thoughts and feelings? Pain-in-the-neck Tudor Melling seems to know, and, much to her surprise, to care.

When Tudor and Rhian set out together to solve the mystery of Bethan's disappearance, their journey of discovery transforms their lives forever.

ISBN 1 85902 696 6

£3.95

Old Enough and other stories

chosen by Christine Evans

Old Enough to . . . make decisions and sometimes make mistakes, to take liberties and take risks, to face challenges but also to face the consequences? At the very least, the young people in these stories are old enough to make discoveries about themselves and are often taken by surprise by what they find . . .

Fifteen new stories from a group of such accomplished writers make *Old Enough* compelling reading.

The contributors are: Stephen Bowkett, Nicola Davies, Malachy Doyle, Catherine Fisher, Catherine Johnson, Paul Lewis, Steve Lockley, Julie Rainsbury, Brian Smith, Jenny Sullivan, Aeres Twigg and Guinevere Vaughan.

'This collection is a cracker, something here for everyone and not a dud amongst them.'—*Jan Mark*

ISBN 1 85902 418 1

£4.50

Rhian's Song

Gillian Drake

Wasn't it enough to hate school and have your best friend move away, without someone invading your favourite space as well? When fifteen-year-old Rhian finds her secret retreat occupied by surly would-be musician Alun Hughes, she decides to abandon the place – leave it for the Welsh weirdo to hide away from *his* problems.

But her town is a small one, and once you know people it's not easy to ignore them. There's Dean Richards, who was at infants school with Rhian – busy making a name for himself in car-stealing and other crime; there are the oldies who befriended Rhian on the beach and whose kindness draw her into their world of crafts and eisteddfodau; there are the dropout Travellers with whom Rhian takes a completely unplanned ride …

Turning tides, shifting sand

Rhian's song, all summer long, tells of change and new beginnings.

'Well-balanced, readable and refreshing.'—*The Guardian.*

ISBN 1 85902 575 7

£4.50

Landlocked

Catherine Johnson

Last days of school . . . that final exam . . . the awkward visit to say goodbye to some of the teachers. Where will it all lead?

Iestyn can't be sure. Plotting a definite course is not his thing. For him, there's more life in charging around the forestry in his mate's car. Until the crash, that is. Until his mate takes up with Martine. Until Iestyn himself has his new job to worry about—and until, more unexpectedly, someone moves in on his feelings with such force that his world is turned upside down.

'A superb book . . . she has captured her teenage protagonists so clearly and imaginatively that they become more real than in any book I have read in a long time.'—*The School Librarian*

ISBN 1 85902 664 8

£3.95

Maddocks

Peter Oram

. . . For a long while he sat, doing nothing at all, gazing out through the gap in the tangle of branches to the wide and silver sea. Charlie, Owen, David, his mother circled slowly round his mind like painted wooden figures on a roundabout . . . the only reality was out there, the shimmering expanse of water that dissolved all hurt, that beckoned him constantly westwards.

. . . The ship cut through the black skin of the sea, scattering stars, its wake of whispering foam following behind like the tail of a comet and glowing with a milky pallor even in the moonless night. All on board were asleep, save the man at the helm, for there was a good, warm wind to fill the sail and the oars could rest.

This is a story of two young men, and maybe many more, who had to strike out on their own for destinations unknown. It is a tale of loneliness and rejection, and of the gnawing pain that comes from believing your family would seem complete without you. What Maddocks and Madog find as they forge their way westwards, over land and over sea, is that the search for oneself is the greatest journey of all.

Peter Oram is a former musician, linguist and teacher who has recently turned to writing—poetry, short stories and this, his first full-length novel. He was born in Cardiff and now lives in west Wales.

'The story is told with effective dash and vividness. It should fascinate every young person with dreams of doing a runner.'—*Books for Keeps*

ISBN 1 85902 669 9

£4.95